KINGS OF RUIN: ADVENTURE IN MUSIC CITY

Praise for Sam Cameron's Work

Mystery of the Tempest is…"Fast, fun, and a great beach read."
—Kristin Cashore, New York Times bestselling novelist

"Intrigue that will delight genre enthusiasts…[*Mystery of the Tempest*] is a true mystery with something to offer teens of any orientation."—*Kirkus Reviews*

The Secret of Othello is…"A lively teen drama with Steven and Denny's practical, caring, sometimes antagonistic and often humorous brotherly relationship at its center."—*Kirkus Reviews*

"*Mystery of the Tempest* is brilliantly conceived and executed. The characters literally jump off the page and into your heart. A funny, thrilling, authentic young adult novel in the Fisher Key Adventure series. I can't wait for the next installment."—Julie Anne Peters, author of *Luna* and *Keeping You a Secret*

Mystery of the Tempest has…"Danger, mystery, suspense, romance, conflict, and teen angst woven into a plot that speeds along complete with crackling dialogue—what more could a reader want? You'll be hooked from the tense opening scene, and after you turn the last page, you'll eagerly await the sequel. Sam Cameron's writing is a gift to teens, past and present. Thoroughly enjoyable."—Lesléa Newman, author of *Heather Has Two Mommies* and *A Letter to Harvey Milk*

By the Author

Kings of Ruin: Adventure in Music City

The Fisher Key Adventures:

Mystery of the Tempest

The Secret of Othello

KINGS OF RUIN: ADVENTURE IN MUSIC CITY

by

Sam Cameron

2013

KINGS OF RUIN: ADVENTURE IN MUSIC CITY

ISBN 10: 1-60282-864-4
ISBN 13: 978-1-60282-864-3

This Trade Paperback Original Is Published By
Bold Strokes Books, Inc.
P.O. Box 249
Valley Falls, NY 12185

First Edition: March 2013

Credits

Editors: Greg Herren & Cindy Cresap
Production Design: Susan Ramundo
Cover Design By Sheri (graphicartist2020@hotmail.com)

PROLOGUE

This is how Danny Kelly's father and brother died: a rainy afternoon in San Francisco, a busy intersection, a green Pontiac Firebird that raced past a red light and T-boned into a gray Toyota Corolla. Danny was home and safe at the time, just eight years old. Much later, he read that broadside collisions were statistically more likely to kill people than any other kind of accident. His mother assured him plenty of times that his father hadn't been at fault. Danny believed her. He did wonder if things might have been different if Dad had been just a little better behind the wheel. Faster. Smarter.

By age twelve, he had learned how to drive from a cute older boy in his neighborhood. A year later, he was joyriding in stolen cars and trying to kiss that same boy, who dressed in leather jackets and drove with wild eyes.

A year after that, everything came crashing to a halt. Literally. Red lights, ambulance sirens, safety glass scattered on the asphalt and splattered with blood. Mom had to hire a lawyer and Danny had to go to court. He told everyone he'd learned his lesson.

The real lesson, though?

Don't get caught.

❖

And this is how Kevin's mother died, way back when, on a lonely stretch of highway between Las Vegas and Los Angeles. He wasn't there, of course. He couldn't know it. But this is true: His parents, John and Maddie Clark, were on their way back to California in a vintage Ford Mustang coupe. Music by the Rolling Stones pounded out of the speakers and past the open windows. The sun was bright and the road endless. They were just a few years out of high school, both of them, young and happy under the desert sun.

"Don't you want to slow down a little?" Maddie shouted over the music.

John glanced down at the speedometer and eased off the pedal. He reached over to squeeze Maddie's knee. "Sorry."

Maddie slid closer to him and gave him a kiss. "I hope Kevin was good for your mom."

The Mustang's steering wheel tugged a little bit under his hands. John frowned. He was a mechanic by trade, and the car was on loan from a friend. He heard another sound, almost like a growl.

Maddie asked, "What's wrong?"

"Nothing," John said just as the pedal dropped out from under his foot and pressed down on its own. They'd been cruising at seventy mph, but now the needle swung to eighty, and then ninety, and made a fast sweep toward one hundred—

"Slow down!" Maddie yelled.

"I'm trying!" John yelled back.

The steering wheel jerked. The Mustang flipped.

The roof smashed against the asphalt. The windshield and every other window shattered. Momentum lifted the car, flipped her again, and dashed her down like a discarded toy. The tires blew out and the frame tore itself apart.

Quiet settled over the mangled mess of metal and blood. Oil trickled out of the cracked-open engine, and broken glass twinkled in the bright sunlight. Maddie was already dead. John survived, just barely, with shattered bones and a broken heart.

These days, Kevin barely remembered his mom at all—just fragments of the songs she used to sing and the perfume she used to wear. But he knew his dad had never forgotten. His dad, who gave up everything—his job as a mechanic, their home in the suburbs, a normal life—to drag Kevin around the country on a long, hard quest.

Meanwhile, the thing that had caused the Mustang's accident happily hopped into John's ambulance to hitchhike back to Las Vegas. It liked Vegas. Lots of cars there; lots of steel to smash.

Lots of things to Ruin.

Briefing Report
Department of Transportation: TOP SECRET

King #1—Signature Code 1832D: Location unknown
King #2—Signature Code 2072F: Team on site Miami FL
King #3—Signature Code 3854D: Last seen Oakland CA
King #4—Signature Code 4211O: Location unknown
King #6—Signature Code 6198D: Terminated
King #7—Signature Code 7892F: Last seen Boston MA
King #8—Signature Code 8078A: Location unknown

King #5: Signature Code 5699D:
Escaped Dallas TX

POSSIBLE DETECTION
Nashville, TN.

CHAPTER ONE

"All I need is two tickets to Country Harvest," said the tall kid standing between Danny and his lunch. "I hear you can get some."

Danny's stomach ached with hunger, and the tie around his neck was trying to strangle him. He really hated private school uniforms. "You heard wrong."

Ryan Woods reached for his wallet. "I know it's been sold out for months, but it's really important. It's for my mom."

Danny understood what it was like to be desperate for a birthday gift for your own mother. He'd had a few close calls himself over the years. But Ryan was asking for the impossible, and Danny's pizza was getting cold on his blue plastic tray.

"Sorry," he said and tried to go around.

Ryan grabbed his arm. "I can pay whatever you want!"

Danny was short but strong and he knew how to fight, if he had to. "Let me go," he growled.

Ryan's grip released. "Come on. Just two tickets?"

Danny stepped past him and into the large, sunny cafeteria of Piedmont Prep, where a hundred students in identical blue blazers were talking and laughing in their little cliques. Even after two months in this new school outside Nashville, Danny still felt like a stranger. His friend Eric had already grabbed a table and was motioning him over.

"You're late," Eric said, his mouth full of French fries. "Did Ryan Woods find you?"

Danny dropped to the bench. "I can't help him."

"Why not? Your stepdad's in charge of the whole weekend." Eric dipped more fries into ketchup. "Twenty thousand screaming country-western fans eating barbeque, drinking beer, and standing in line for ten hours to get a single autograph. I know it offends your city boy, rock 'n' roll image and all, but you might like it."

Danny lifted his hamburger. "I'd rather ram screwdrivers through my eyeballs."

"You say that now, but you'll get used to it."

No, he wouldn't. There were a lot of things he wasn't going to get used to about life in Tennessee. The twang in people's accents, for starters. Grown men and women wearing cowboy hats. The stupid school uniforms and his stupid tie. He loosened the knot.

Eric warned him, "That's a demerit if you get caught."

Danny shrugged. "Wouldn't be my first."

"How was your progress report?"

Danny winced. He didn't know how he was going to explain a C in English to his mother or stepdad. He'd had to spend the first half of his lunch period listening to his teacher tell him that he could do better if he tried harder. Same stuff he'd heard back in school in San Francisco.

"That good, huh?" Eric asked. "You going to get grounded for your birthday?"

A small hand fell on Danny's shoulder before he could answer. He turned to see Laura Lewis standing behind him. Laura was tiny and pretty, with a heart-shaped face and wispy blond hair always done up in a ponytail. Twice a week, she took dance class at the studio next to Zinc's Sandwiches and came in afterward to see him. She was only a freshman, but that was okay.

"Hey, Danny," she said. "I brought you something."

In her hands she held a chocolate cupcake decorated with the number "16" in blue frosting.

"I know your birthday's not until Sunday, but here you go," she said.

Danny knew he should kiss her. That's what you did when girlfriends brought you things. No one at Piedmont Prep knew that Danny liked boys. They never would. All he had to do was keep lying to Laura and Eric and everyone else. He pushed down his guilty conscience.

"Thanks," he said. "Are you coming over tonight?"

She sighed. "My sister wants me to babysit. I told her that I couldn't, but she did this guilt thing and now I'm stuck with the twins all night. She won't let me have company. Are you working tomorrow?"

"Supposed to."

Laura smiled. "I guess that means you'll have to come see me at Country Harvest on Sunday. My dad's playing on stage, and everyone will be there, and it's a really good time even if you don't love country music."

"It's not that I don't love it," Danny said. "It's just, you know…not my thing."

"Tell her about the screwdrivers," Eric said.

The bell rang, ending the lunch period. Laura put the cupcake in Danny's hand and said, "Call me later."

As she turned away, he touched her arm and did the kissing thing, but only on the cheek. "Thanks again for the cupcake."

"Mr. Kelly!" That was the stern voice of Mr. Woodbury. "I saw that."

Laura grinned and ducked away in the crowd of students heading for the door. Eric stood up with his lunch tray and said, "See you later, birthday boy."

Mr. Woodbury took a long time writing the demerit up in his little black book. Danny had to race to his locker and grab his physics book. He was too busy to glance out the windows, but if he had, he would have seen the October sun shining down on a hundred sleek, gleaming vehicles.

In the middle of the lot, amid the steel and plastic and leather, a brand-new yellow Porsche 911 with the license plate JRMOON1 rolled forward a few feet. No one was there to see it. The headlights blinked on and blinked off. The windshield wipers flicked once as a growl came from beneath the hood.

The car rolled back into place.

There was no driver behind the wheel.

CHAPTER TWO

Mr. Mendoza, Danny's physics teacher, had not come in that Friday. The class had a substitute teacher who stood in front of the classroom like an army general addressing the troops. This particular general just happened to be wearing a crisp white business suit and black high heels. Her hair was as dark as her shoes and hung around her face like a shoulder-length silk scarf.

She was easily the most beautiful woman Danny had ever seen. If it weren't for the whole gay thing, he might have fallen a little bit in love with her right then and there.

"—which is why, ladies and gentlemen, physics is the means, not the end, to understand engineering." The teacher had a clipped accent he didn't recognize. Not quite British, but not Australian. South African? She stopped her lecture to focus on him in the doorway and didn't even consult the seating chart in her hand. "Mr. Kelly. Please join us."

In the first row, Rachel Anderson gave Danny a smirk. Petite and perfect, she was always happy when he got into trouble. He'd never had a stepsister before, but surely, they weren't all as aggravating as she was.

He slunk toward his assigned chair in the third row. As he sat he banged his knee against the underside and stifled a curse. The girls around him snickered. Most of the time they ignored him just as he ignored physics. It was more fun to doodle lyrics in the margins of his notebook, songs for his band, The Dirty Hands.

Danny didn't think he was going to get any doodling done today, though.

The substitute teacher rapped on Mr. Mendoza's desk with the edge of her pen and gave everyone a stern look. Behind her, the name MRS. MORRIS had been written across the whiteboard in large black letters.

"You will fail every important task in your life if you don't understand engineering," Mrs. Morris announced. "You will fail in your occupations, fail in your relationships, and fail in your personal fortunes. Engineering is not about dull science and even duller scientists. The most important thing you'll ever learn is how to build and maintain machines, corporations, rules, systems, and relationships. Mr. Conway, who said that an object at rest tends to stay at rest?"

Mitchell Conway Junior, son of the famous country singer Mitchell "Moon" Conway, squirmed in his seat. He was a football player, very handsome, and totally Danny's type if Danny liked them big and dumb.

Which he didn't.

"Newton," someone whispered from behind Junior.

"Newton?" Junior repeated hopefully.

Mrs. Morris was merciless. "And what did he mean by that?"

Junior squirmed some more. Everyone knew that he never did his own homework, never wrote his own papers, and planned on being as big and famous as his father. He wasn't much of a singer, but in Nashville who you knew was more important than how many notes you could sing.

"Something about an object at rest," Junior said, with all eyes in the class focused on him. He brightened. "Does that mean it's naptime?"

The class laughed. Mrs. Morris stalked straight toward Junior's desk. She leaned so close to his face that she could probably smell his breath. Danny bet that it smelled like onions.

"If you don't understand the law of motion, you will fail," Mrs. Morris repeated. "If you don't understand Newton, you will fail. There is no exception. There is no reprieve. Only failure."

Junior leaned back, blanching.

Danny was listening to her words but was paying more attention to the color of her lips, the way her hair swung just over her shoulders, and the shape of her under her suit. She really knew how to dress for success. Was it too gay for him to even think that way? He didn't know. She had the boys in the room transfixed, while the girls looked resentful.

Rachel spoke up in a cold voice. "Isaac Newton believed that you could turn lead into gold. He kept crazy notebooks in code and never even had a girlfriend. Why listen to him?"

Mrs. Morris straightened up and turned toward Rachel. "You must focus on the knowledge itself, not the bearer of it. I've seen men crippled because they didn't understand the relationship between acceleration and mass. I've seen men die because they didn't understand that entropy is an irreversible, inexorable process."

Rachel shrugged and deliberately looked away.

Mrs. Morris swiveled her gaze across several desks and fixed it on Danny.

"Do you understand entropy, Mr. Kelly?"

He hated being called out. So humiliating, even when he knew the answer. His heart pounded uncomfortably hard against his ribs.

"Every closed system decays," he finally managed to say. "Energy moves from organized to unorganized states. Systems fall apart."

"Exactly." Mrs. Morris gave him a small, secret smile. "Maybe you won't be one of the failures, then. In fact, I suspect you have a bright and promising future ahead of you."

He wondered if she had a handsome gay brother somewhere.

CHAPTER THREE

Soon everyone at Piedmont Prep was talking about Mrs. Morris. In gym class, Danny heard that she was some kind of spy sent by the Tennessee Bureau of Education. In the hallway, he heard that she was really not a teacher after all, but instead an actress undercover for some role in a big Hollywood film. By the time the two thirty dismissal bell rang, he'd heard all sorts of rumors. None of them seemed more likely than the other.

Danny grabbed his books for the weekend and met Eric in the parking lot.

"So that's her, huh?" Eric asked as they wound their way past buses and cars. "I hear she's starting some new reality show on TV."

Danny followed Eric's gaze to where Mrs. Morris was pacing back and forth on the sidewalk, talking on a surprisingly large cell phone. Any time a student approached her, she turned and walked the other way in animated conversation.

"She's certainly not the lunch lady," Danny agreed.

A voice from nearby said, "Hey, better go get your girlfriend, Kelly, before she gets herself a new boy toy. Everyone knows about those teachers having sex with dweeby losers."

Danny turned to Junior Conway and his knot of friends, who were lingering around Junior's brand new yellow Porsche 911. Rachel was with him, text messaging on her phone. Junior was leering at Mrs. Morris.

Danny said, "As a matter of fact, we're running off to Tahiti tomorrow. Leaving on a jet plane."

"Too bad you can't drive her to Tahiti."

"Yeah, because cars do so well underwater," Danny retorted.

Junior's face turned red. "Because you don't have a car, moron. Where's your ride? Nowhere. And even if you had something to drive, it would be nothing compared to mine. Get it? Nowhere and nothing."

Danny walked over to Junior's Porsche. Everyone knew how Moon Conway Sr. had bought it for Junior's birthday a week ago. It was shiny and bright and maybe good enough for most, but Danny gave it a dismissive glance.

"Anyone can get a Porsche," he said. "If you knew anything about cars, you'd get yourself a Bugatti Veyron sixteen point four."

Rachel ended her phone call and tossed her hair over her shoulder. "Ignore him, Junior. He doesn't know what he's talking about."

Danny folded his arms. "The Bugatti goes from zero to sixty in two point six seconds. It tops out at two hundred fifty miles an hour. It's got an eight liter, sixty-four valve, quad turbo engine, and carbon-ceramic brakes that can bring it from top speed to a dead stop in under ten seconds. How good's a Porsche now?"

Junior glared at him. "You ain't ever going to own a Bug-whatever."

"I don't want to own it," Danny said. "But one day I'm going to drive it. Which is more than you're ever going to do."

He walked back toward Eric's black Camaro coupe, which was certainly not a Porsche and nowhere near a Bugatti, but nonetheless, a reliable machine. Eric was leaning against the driver's doorframe, his sunglasses halfway down his nose.

Eric asked, "You done poking at Junior?"

"Yeah," Danny said. "Can I drive?"

"No. Get in the car, Mr. Bugatti."

Danny yanked off the hated tie, pulled off his jacket, and tossed both in the back before sliding into the passenger seat.

Making fun of Junior was a little risky, especially since Roger
Rat was the vice president of Moon's label, and his mom was
now a publicist for the same company. But some days he just
couldn't stop himself.

"All right, where to, birthday boy?" Eric asked as he wedged
himself behind the wheel. "My treat. Golf? Bowling? We've got
all of this fine afternoon. And if you're really feeling adventurous,
the big Piedmont-Waltham football game is tonight. We can go
mock big guys with tiny brains."

"Drive out to Highway Twelve and let me race for a while."

"I can't." Eric turned the ignition. "You know my mom's
got one of those GPS things in this car. She checks up on me all
the time."

Danny watched Mrs. Morris pace more with her cell phone.
He wondered who she was talking to so passionately. She was
making long sweeps of the sidewalk now, stalking back and forth
in her high heels.

"If you're not going to let me race, take me on home,"
Danny said.

"Home!" Eric turned on the radio and blasted some good
old-fashioned Aerosmith. "What are you, Mr. Dead Boring? Mr.
Zero Adventure?"

"I've got music to write." Danny turned the stereo down and
pulled out the lyrics he'd been working on. "All right, how's this:
'Your lips so bright, your words so right, you are the apple of my
eye.'"

Eric steered into the long line of cars waiting to pass by the
football field. Piedmont had two fields, plus a new field house,
and a gymnasium with large screen video monitors. "To what
song?" he asked.

"It's a new one."

"You can't start a new song until you finish the last song.
Band rule."

Danny tapped his pencil against the car door. "My last song
sucks."

Eric said, "You liked it last week."

"The goddess of inspiration is fickle."

"I'm going to inspirationally kick your butt," Eric grumbled, but he didn't sound too upset about it. Until they got a new drummer, it was just the two of them in The Dirty Hands, and they could change the rules whenever they wanted. "How fickle is this—my mom's going to take my keys away if I don't lose ten pounds."

Danny blinked at him, the lyrics momentarily forgotten. "That's cruel."

Eric patted his sizeable belly, which stretched the buttons of his button-down shirt. "Baby fat. But I'm no baby, she says. Talk about cruel, though. You're the only kid at Piedmont who's going to celebrate his sixteenth birthday without a brand-new driver's license. People are going to talk."

"So what."

"And I'm the only one who knows the truth why."

"I shouldn't have told you."

"But you did." Eric gloated. "You and your criminal mastermind past."

"Shut up," Danny said.

Ten minutes later, Eric turned on to Danny's street. Danny was back to work on the lyrics, trying to think up a rhyme for "hair," when he heard Eric's appreciative whistle.

"Maybe this is your lucky day after all," Eric said.

Danny looked up. The Anderson household—Roger Rat's house—was one of the largest on the block, an all-brick extravagance with high windows, creeping ivy, and a lawn big enough to hold a marching band. Parked in the circular driveway was a brand-new, all black Dakota Laramie truck with a crew cab and chrome moldings.

Tied across the gleaming black hood was a giant red gift ribbon.

CHAPTER FOUR

K evin Clark thought that maybe, just maybe, someone had once loved the little Mazda Protégé he was currently driving—someone who might have moisturized the dry, cracked dashboard, or vacuumed the dirty mats, or waxed the now-faded blue exterior. Someone must have enjoyed it back when it smelled like new plastic and not like mold. But whoever that mythical owner had been, whoever might have once owned and cared for the car, that person was long gone. Instead, there was only Kevin to argue with the sticky gear stick and fight the steering wheel, which tended to pull to the left.

"Piece of crap car," he said, and then regretted it. He patted the steering column. "Sorry. Not your fault, right?"

Steering the Mazda into the parking lot at Piedmont Prep made Kevin feel uncomfortable. All those nice cars, and all those rich kids, and here he was like some country bumpkin in the middle of the big city. Except suburban Nashville wasn't quite the big city, and no student with half a brain could mistake Kevin's leather coat and jeans for faded farmers' coveralls.

Besides, who wanted to live these lives? Stuck in school all year long, planning ahead to safe, predictable careers, never seeing the America he knew or the evil that ran amuck in it. Never making a difference like Kevin and his father and everyone else who worked to eradicate the Ruins.

He backed the Mazda into a slot at the end of the lot and killed the engine. No need to waste gasoline and spew exhaust into the atmosphere. He pulled a small silver box out of the glove compartment and set it up on the dashboard. The exterior looked like a satellite radio receiver, but the inside was one of the most sophisticated pieces of surveillance equipment ever invented by the scientists at the Department of Transportation.

Zoron readings flashed by on the screen as students exited the parking lot: 22, 21, 18, 23. The one nice thing about the Mazda was that it was a flat, perfect 0. Kevin had fried it himself. No chance of a Ruin under this hood, thanks anyway. A Honda Civic passed with a nice low 12; the Chevy Blazer following it was a 25.

"I could get the same readings at the mall," he told the Mazda. Not that he liked shopping. He wished he were on his motorcycle, zooming free across the desert.

Anywhere but a high school parking lot.

Then again, if that Ruin King from Dallas *was* here, he'd personally zap every car in town in order to kill it.

An hour's worth of surveillance later, his butt was numb from the lopsided seat, and most of the lot was empty. Mrs. Morris, who'd been scanning with her FRED from the sidewalk, slid into the passenger seat.

"This was pretty worthless," Kevin said.

"I agree." Mrs. Morris kicked off her high heels. "Like most Kings, it's a smart one. Knows how to disguise itself when it's not active. It could have passed right by either one of us and not registered more than a ten or twenty."

"So what do we do now?"

"Let's get some ice cream. I'm starving."

Kevin turned the ignition. A terrible screech from under the hood announced the fan belt's impending demise. "Did you have fun teaching all day?"

Mrs. Morris leaned her head back. "Just as much fun as teaching you, multiplied by a hundred."

Though it was cool outside, autumn turning the trees red and gold, Kevin found an open ice cream shop and got them both chocolate cones. The guy at the counter was his own age, with spiky brown hair and a ring through his left eyebrow. Not quite Kevin's type. If he had a type. If he had a love life. Moving around so much made relationships hard.

Not that he was brooding or anything.

"You could ask him to a movie," Mrs. Morris said when they were outside.

"And then leave town tomorrow or the next day," Kevin said. "Not very nice."

"Believe it or not, he might not be looking to settle down at age seventeen," she replied.

He shrugged. "Not worth the effort."

She faced him and affectionately brushed his bangs out of his eyes.

"You are totally worth the effort," she said.

They were still eating their ice cream when they reached Spike's Junk and Auto Parts. The yard was an enormous sprawl of junked cars, discarded tires, and scrap metal. Richie Venezuela, the middle-aged owner, was sitting on the front steps of the office with an orange tabby cat rubbing at his foot.

"How'd she run?" Richie asked as Kevin tossed him the Mazda's keys.

"Fan belt's ripping apart," he said. "Also needs new shocks, and that muffler's going to fall off any minute."

"You should buy her." Richie hauled himself to his feet. "I'll give you a good deal."

Kevin had grown up around salesmen, mechanics, and entrepreneurs like Richie. The Society of Free Mechanics was an enormously useful volunteer organization, but you couldn't trust half of them with your wallet or your pink slip.

"Mr. Venezuela," he said, "you couldn't pay me to give that car to my worst enemy."

He spread his hands. "You break my heart, kid. Did you find that King?"

Mrs. Morris asked, "Are you sure what you saw?"

Richie sat down again. "I told you! I'm up there to tow some teacher last week, and the scanner hit ninety! It fit that signature profile from Dallas perfectly."

Mrs. Morris gazed at him steadily from behind her sunglasses. Kevin bent to pet Spike, the orange cat the junkyard was named after. Spike rubbed up against his hand, sniffed for non-existent treats, and purred loudly.

"We didn't find it," Mrs. Morris said. "I was very disappointed."

Mrs. Morris headed for the battered-looking RV parked behind the office. Kevin said, "It's not good when she's disappointed," and followed his teammate to the Pit, their mobile headquarters.

On the outside, it looked like any twenty-eight foot long travel trailer that spent half the year in some driveway and the other half hauling Mom, Dad, and a handful of kids around the country to national parks. The seven-foot ceilings, high definition TV, and wooden ceiling fans inside weren't especially unique. But one entire wall was covered with a cabinet holding high-tech computer consoles, radio equipment, and special sensors. Another cabinet contained their weapons and scanners. The bunkroom slept all four members of the team as well as their German shepherds, Apollo and Zeus. There were two bathrooms, a good thing when you were on the road for ten months a year.

The Pit was more than just an RV. It was Kevin's home, and had been for as long as he could remember.

Mrs. Morris headed for the stove to make tea. Zeus and Apollo, roused from their naps, nuzzled Kevin's hands for attention. Gear, who'd been up on the roof working on the satellite dish, poked his head down through the hatch.

"Find anything?" he asked.

"Utter waste of time," Mrs. Morris said.

Gear dropped down to the carpet. He was the tallest man Kevin had ever known—tall, black, and muscled. He could do a hundred one-handed push-ups without breaking a sweat or taking off his small silver glasses. He was better with their equipment than anyone else, but after years of practice, Kevin was a close second.

"Where's my dad?" Kevin asked, snagging an apple from a bowl.

"Went sniffing on his own," Gear said.

"No headaches?" Mrs. Morris asked, because everyone knew John Clark, code named Ford, was still recuperating from the Dallas incident.

"Not that he would admit to. He took the Harley."

Ford had a 1986 black low rider that he treated like gold. Kevin owned his own blue Kawasaki Vulcan. Mrs. Morris kept a classic Mercedes-Benz in storage along with her other antique automobiles. Gear didn't own any cars, but drove whatever loaners they got on a job, or rode a ten-speed bicycle just for fun.

Kevin didn't want to think about his father out there somewhere, riding around when he should really be resting. "What now? If Mr. Venezuela really did see a car spike up at Piedmont Prep, we didn't find it today."

Mrs. Morris withdrew a tiny computer drive from her pocket. "Luckily, I was able to access the parking permit files from the school office. We're going to comb through them, cross-referencing names and cars and the scans we took today. Maybe someone was absent."

Research. Kevin was good at it, but didn't have to like it. "That's all?"

Gear said, "After we do that, you can get out your cheer-leading pom-poms."

Kevin replied, "Don't even go there."

"Big game tonight," Gear said with a grin. "Piedmont Prep versus Waltham High. We're going to inspect every car in that parking lot. If there's a Ruin King hiding out in this town, we're going to find it."

Or die trying, Kevin almost added. *Just like Dallas.*

CHAPTER FIVE

Y ou better call me," Eric said as Danny slammed the door. "Like, in ten minutes."

"I'll call," Danny promised him.

Eric backed out of the driveway, blasted his horn a couple of times, and zoomed off. Danny gingerly approached the Dakota parked by the front door. The truck was so clean and gleaming it reflected the house, the trees, even the sky above. Through the driver's window he could see leather-trimmed bucket seats and state-of-the-art stereo and navigation systems.

The keys were in the ignition.

Hoping against hope, he pushed the front door open.

He didn't know how he should react to his mother's unexpected generosity. Play it cool? Throw his arms around her and lift her off the ground? Nothing she'd ever done before had been so amazing. He could almost forgive her for all the rotten stuff with Roger and moving out here. No, forget almost. He would definitely forgive her. For every single thing and more.

He would maybe even forgive Roger. A little bit.

"Mom?" he asked, trekking down the large hall. A box of Halloween decorations was sitting outside Roger's office. Danny didn't care much about Halloween anymore, though he liked getting candy. The walls above the box were decorated with framed photos of Roger with country-western stars—new celebrities like Moon Conway and older ones like Willie Nelson. "You home?"

"In here," she called out from the kitchen.

The kitchen was Danny's least favorite part of the house—too white, too large, and too cold. His mother was standing at the sink, straining macaroni through a colander. She was dressed for work in high-heeled cowboy boots and a crisp blue blouse. Her cell phone was cradled to her ear.

"Yes, we can do that interview on Sunday. But it'll have to be on the bus as we're heading down to the Opry. Moon's schedule is very busy."

Danny dropped his backpack on the floor just as Comet trotted out of the sunroom and around the kitchen island. He was an old terrier, his dark hair shot through with gray, and if he didn't quite bounce up and down against Danny's leg the way he used to, he wagged his tail and nuzzled Danny's shoes.

"All right, call me back." Mom hung up the phone and carried the colander to a large glass bowl. "Hi, honey. Did you see the truck?"

"Yeah." He dumped his backpack on the floor, and opened his arms to give her a giant hug. "It's amazing."

"Roger's boss even personalized the plates for him. MUZKBUX. Music bucks." She dropped the now-empty colander in the sink and ran water through it. "The insurance won't come through until tomorrow, though."

Danny dropped his arms. "Roger's boss bought him a truck?"

A timer went off on the stove. Mom slid past Danny to rescue a covered casserole from the oven.

"His bonus this year," she said. "He told us, remember?"

Danny's knees felt weak. He sat on the nearest stool. "No, he didn't."

"I'm sure he did." Mom looked closely at him. "You didn't think—"

"Sunday's my birthday," he said.

She shook her head. "Danny. The deal hasn't changed. You agreed to it in front of Judge Hensel."

"A lot of other things changed." He couldn't keep the resentment out of his voice. "Why not that? I didn't ask to be dragged out of California or go to some stupid private school."

She crossed her arms. "Isn't today progress report day, young man?"

Danny said, "That's not what we're talking about!"

The doorbell rang. Mom glanced toward the front of the house. "That's Amanda with the press schedule. We'll talk about this later. Leave your grades on the table."

She went to answer the door. Danny yanked the report from his backpack, slapped it on the kitchen island, and stalked upstairs with Comet close at heel. He shut his bedroom door louder than he was supposed to. From his window, he could see Roger Rat's brand new truck, mocking him from the driveway. Roger already owned a Mercedes S550, which cost a lot more than a brand-new pickup. MUZKBUX, indeed.

He glanced at the wall and the framed picture of himself, his dad, and his brother Mickey. In the photo, Danny was just a little kid. Both Mickey and Danny were wearing baseball gloves. The photo had been taken at Giants Stadium just a week before the accident.

Before Dad and Mickey were killed in a senseless car accident.

Comet, sitting on the bed, tilted his head and made a soft noise in his throat.

"I know." Danny scratched the dog's ear. "But who wants a stupid hillbilly truck, anyway?"

CHAPTER SIX

K evin's father was standing on the flat roof of Richie Venezuela's garage, peering into the night. His hands were jammed into his pockets, and he didn't seem to notice the chill air. Down below, traffic snaked through the prosperous suburban streets. Nashville, the city of dreams, was a golden glow in the low northern clouds.

Kevin didn't see what was so fascinating about cities. He preferred the open road under a blazing Midwest sky. October nights in Tennessee were colder than he'd thought, and he shivered in the cold wind.

"The reports are ready," he said from behind his father. "Everything we scanned in the Piedmont Prep parking lot cross-referenced against the parking permit records."

"Okay," he said.

He sounded preoccupied. Thinking about the Ruins out there, no doubt. Kevin was sure that was all he thought about, day and night.

"And there's some dinner," he added. Mexican fast food, which he and Gear loved and Mrs. Morris pretended to hate.

Kevin heard footsteps behind them and turned to see Mrs. Morris coming up the stairs. The older woman had changed into jeans and a football sweatshirt and bright white sneakers. Free of makeup, her black hair pulled back with a beaded headband, she could have been twenty years old, Kevin's older sister. But unlike Kevin, she was glamorous and brilliant and could have any boyfriend she wanted.

"What's he doing?" Mrs. Morris asked.

"Brooding," Kevin said.

Mrs. Morris joined Ford out on the roof. Kevin retreated a few feet, fully intending to give them their privacy, but curiosity made him linger.

"See something fascinating?" Mrs. Morris asked.

"It's out there somewhere," Ford said, his eyes still on the city.

Mrs. Morris didn't seem impressed by that announcement. "So we suspect."

"This isn't going to be Dallas all over again," he said. "I promise you that."

Kevin felt his cheeks turn red.

"People make mistakes," Mrs. Morris said. "You have to let it go."

Ford shook his head.

Kevin fled down the stairs. He didn't need to hear more about how disappointed his dad was in him. It was his fault that King #5 had escaped Dallas. His fault it was here in Nashville, and more people could die.

He grabbed his jacket and helmet and climbed on his Kawasaki.

"Where are you going?" Gear asked. "We've got tacos!"

"I'm not hungry," Kevin said and drove off.

His dad's blame hurt Kevin, but the blame he placed on himself hurt much, much worse.

CHAPTER SEVEN

Dinner was excruciating.

It was bad enough that Danny had to endure Mom and Roger Rat's disapproval of his English grade in addition to Roger gloating over his new truck, but Rachel's unexpected presence made things even worse. She wasn't supposed to be over this weekend, but her mother was dating some new guy, and so custody weekends had become a lot more flexible.

Rachel, annoyingly enough, had all A's on her progress report.

"It's not hard if you do your homework and pay attention in class instead of writing songs," she said.

Mom gave Danny a sharp look. "Are you writing music in class?"

"No." Danny gulped at some soda. "Only when it's boring."

Roger was sawing through his steak with a knife. He was tall and slim and Mom called him handsome, but Danny thought his nose was too wide and his forehead too high. Roger said, "Maybe we should think about no guitar until your grades come up."

Danny almost dropped his glass. "What?"

Quickly, Mom said, "We'd have to talk about that."

Talk about that. Danny knew what those words meant. He'd heard them enough over the last year. Roger said something his mother didn't agree with, and so they'd have a fight about it, and Roger would win.

But Roger wasn't going to win this one. Danny was never, ever going to give up the guitar. He'd run away first, hitchhike to California, live on the streets.

Lots of musicians came from the streets, right?

He gave his mother a sharp look.

Mom repeated, "We'll talk about it," and Danny stabbed at his Caesar salad.

After dinner, Mom and Roger put the new truck in the garage and went off in the Mercedes to a publicity party for Country Harvest. Danny went up to his room. He tried texting Eric, but there was no answer. He tried calling Laura, but she didn't pick up her cell phone. She'd updated her Facebook, though. There was a picture of a shopping bag and the headline "NEW BOOTS!"

Nothing about him, though.

"Looks like it's you and me," he said to Comet, sprawled in a nap on Danny's pillow.

Twenty minutes later, Junior's yellow Porsche pulled into the driveway.

"So what I don't need," Danny said.

The phone rang. One check of the caller ID and he picked up immediately.

"It's the birthday boy!" Morgan shouted. He sounded like he was on a train or bus. "How old are you now, buckaroo?"

An ache of homesickness struck Danny just under the ribs. He flopped down in his chair. "Twenty-five. Send me a gift, jerk."

Morgan laughed. "Yeah, I've got one right here for you. I'm working. Got a job."

"A job doing what?"

"You'll never believe. City Hall!"

"You're working at San Francisco City Hall?" Danny said. "How can that be?"

"Juvenile intervention diversion program. That means rotten kids like me working in office jobs so we can see the other side of life. How's life in hillbilly country? Full of rednecks?"

"Full of rich kids who don't know anything about cars," Danny answered. "And singers who don't know how to sing."

They talked for a half hour, mostly about music and the friends Danny'd had to leave behind, nothing about who Morgan might be dating or sleeping with. Which was okay, actually, because every reminder that Morgan was straight was another kind of ache. *All* the handsome ones were straight. After hanging up, Danny gave up on his book report and headed over to the garage. When he went downstairs, Junior and Rachel were sitting at the kitchen island. Junior was eating out of a salad bowl filled with Cheerios.

"Seriously, how much does one of those bugs cost?" Junior asked.

Danny squinted at him. "What?"

"Those cars. Titanium carbon brakes. Whatever you were talking about today."

Junior's capacity for mangling information was amazing. Danny said, "A million or two. The tires alone are fifty thousand dollars."

"I could get one," Junior said confidently. "My dad would buy me one."

Rachel's hand was on Junior's sleeve, her fingers tapping on his skin. "If you had one, would you let me drive it?"

"Sure." Junior kissed her and got milk on her lips.

Danny rolled his eyes and grabbed a soda from the refrigerator.

"So, seriously, how come you can't drive?" Junior asked.

"I don't want to," Danny said.

"No, really, the whole story," Junior turned to Rachel. "What is it? Loves cars, doesn't want to drive? I'm not that dumb."

Rachel's gaze slid past Junior to Danny. He saw gloating in her expression and figured this was it. By Monday morning, everyone in school would know about his criminal mastermind past.

"You know what they say," she replied scornfully. "Those who can, do. Those who can't just end up talking about cars they're never going to be able to afford. Come on, Junior. We're going to be late for the movies."

On her way out the door, as Junior's Porsche idled outside, Rachel said, "Don't wait up."

Danny replied, "I won't." He jammed his hands in his pockets. "And, you know, thanks. For not telling Junior."

"Whatever. Just don't go joyriding around in my dad's new truck just because he left the keys in the kitchen. He knows that it's only got twenty-seven miles on the odometer."

"I wasn't going to," Danny protested.

She gave him a squinty look and left.

Danny checked the kitchen. The ignition key to MUZKBUX was hanging by the door on a brand-new leather monogram key ring.

He touched the key. The metal was cold against his fingers, and he imagined himself sliding it into the ignition.

CHAPTER EIGHT

No," Danny said to himself. He didn't need to drive Roger Rat's truck, wasn't even going to think about it. He left the key in place. With Comet trotting behind him, he headed out the kitchen door, through the mudroom and into the two-story, three-bay garage. Back in San Francisco, no one had ginormous garages. Danny knew some homeless families that would happily move into this one. He ignored MUZKBUX and his mother's Volvo 680 and went up the carpeted stairs to the loft.

Lots of junk up there, including Christmas decorations and some of their furniture from California, but Danny was slowly turning the place into his own music studio. As a studio, it needed a lot of work. He hadn't figured out a good place to set up the electronic keyboard, and the drums were still disassembled from the move. But the walls were insulated, there was a window overlooking the driveway, and there was plenty of room to buy more guitars.

So far, he owned only two. One was a Gibson electric guitar he'd bought with his own money and the other was a worn, inexpensive acoustic guitar that had been his father's. If Danny squeezed his eyes closed, he could remember Dad sitting with the instrument across his knee, playing in the corner of the living room. Mom had said he wanted to play in coffee shops and fairs, but never had the time.

Danny took the Gibson down from its rack on the wall, set it across his knee, and studied the lyrics he'd started to write about Mrs. Morris. He was trying very hard not to think about MUZKBUX, gleaming and all alone in the garage below.

Your hair so black and fine. . .

His fingers picked out the first new notes. It was going to start slow, build to a crescendo, before ending poignantly. A rock 'n' roll ballad. He paused, looking out the window. A dark car cruised slowly down the street. Maybe a lost pizza delivery guy. Pizza sounded good. He was beginning to regret not eating more at dinner.

Beauty to last until the end of time . . .

In the garage below, MUZKBUX flashed its headlights.

Danny had his back to the stairs and didn't see the light. Comet did, though. The dog padded toward the staircase and barked.

"Hush," Danny said. "I'm working."

Comet sat with his head on his paws, watching alertly.

In the bushes outside, a small remote-controlled beach buggy was also watching. 2KEWLE was its name. It was only six inches long and four inches tall, with a lithium polymer rechargeable battery and DC motor. Following Junior's Porsche here had meant swerving around storm drains, avoiding dogs and cars, and crossing streets full of hazardous traffic.

The trip was worth the danger, though. 2KEWLE knew exactly what had been in the Porsche and was now in Roger Rat's new truck.

Danny's song for Mrs. Morris drifted from the open windows above.

2KEWLE rolled forward a little, listening.

In the garage, MUZKBUX flashed his lights again. King #5 had jumped into the truck from Junior's Porsche, hoping for some adventure. Not music. He decided it was time to leave. A small arc of zoron energy arced out of its headlights and hit the garage door switch.

With a rumble, the doors began to open.

Danny stopped playing his guitar. He hadn't heard Roger and Mom returning, but who else would be opening the garage doors? He crossed to the top of the stairs and peered into the darkness.

"Hello?" he asked. "Who's down there?"

Comet barreled down the stairs. Danny followed, reaching out for the light. When he reached the bottom, he saw MUZKBUX and the Volvo parked exactly where they had been. The garage doors were open for no good reason at all. The street outside was quiet but for the wind pushing autumn leaves around.

All was quiet and normal.

No, wait—something was in the bushes. Small and harmless, but definitely out of place.

"Where'd you come from?" Danny asked. He picked up the toy. With its bright blue exterior and rollover bar, it reminded him of Los Angeles beach buggies. It had a battery compartment but no serial number or other identifying information, other than a tiny license plate that read 2KEWLE.

"Someone must have lost it," Danny said to Comet, who had followed him outside. "It's just a toy."

A bright green spark zapped from the buggy into Danny's hands.

"Ow!" he yelped.

He dropped the toy back into the bushes and inspected his hands. No burns on his palms or fingers, but they tingled.

"Stupid thing," he said.

Down on the ground, 2KEWLE's headlights lit up. His engine turned on and he rolled toward MUZKBUX. Danny watched in amazement. He shivered in the cold air and turned to glare at the dark trees, house, and yard.

"Okay, whoever's out there, this isn't funny. Come out here."

Nobody stepped forward. Danny figured the buggy was radio controlled. Maybe it belonged to a neighbor who had lost it and was trying to get it back home. Didn't they need to see it in order to know how to steer it? He also had no idea how far a range the transmitters had.

He followed 2KEWLE inside the garage. The buggy had gone dark again, no sign of life.

"Okay, fine," Danny said. He wasn't about to pick it up and get zapped again. Instead, he found a cardboard box, turned it upside down, and put it over the vehicle. "You can just stay there for tonight."

He should have shut the garage doors and gone back upstairs to his guitar, but Roger's truck was just sitting there, gleaming in the light. A fine piece of machinery, even if Roger was never going to truly appreciate it. Danny ran his hands over the hood. Smooth and cool. He opened the driver's door. Without the key, he couldn't do much, but the seat was comfortable and his hands fit naturally on the steering wheel.

Comet started barking like crazy.

"What is it, boy?" Danny asked.

From under the cardboard box, 2KEWLE beeped his horn urgently.

Roger's truck roared to life.

Danny jerked back from the wheel. The dashboard lit up and the radio blasted out Moon Senior's latest hit. When the truck started rolling backward, Danny tried the brake, but the pedal was like mush under his foot.

"Oh, no," Danny said. "Stop! What are you doing? Stop!"

He tried opening the door, but it wouldn't open. Instead, the truck backed out of the garage, picked up speed, and gunned down the street with Danny as its prisoner.

CHAPTER NINE

"Stop!" Danny yelled again. He banged his hands against the steering wheel. "What are you doing?"

MUZKBUX reached the end of the street and ran the stop light.

Danny tried everything. He poked at the ignition, pulled on the emergency brake, jammed the gear stick to neutral. Nothing made any difference. He couldn't open the door or even roll down the window, which was just crazy. Surely, no combination of electrical misfires or ignition malfunctions could make that happen.

No matter what happened, he was *so* going to get blamed. He just knew it.

"I need reinforcements," Danny said. He groped for his cell phone, but he'd left it in the studio. He had no way to call for help.

More traffic now, cars and SUVs passing him in the dark. Danny slid the seat belt on. He put both hands on the wheel and pretended he had control. He didn't want to look like an idiot, after all. But now they were approaching a four-way stop sign, and he didn't think MUZKBUX was going to stop at all.

"Stop sign!" he said. "Slow down!"

The truck sped up. Danny squeezed his eyes shut and braced for impact. Brakes squealed and someone blasted their horn angrily, but there was no crunch of metal or sickening thump of impact.

"You are so going to get me killed," he told MUZKBUX. "Where's a cop when you need one?"

The truck swerved onto Crescent Avenue, nearly hitting a rider on a Japanese motorcycle. Another angry horn blasted through the air. Danny threw his hands up helplessly as MUZKBUX gunned for downtown. The motorcycle followed, and within seconds was pulling up beside Danny's door.

"It's not my fault!" Danny yelled.

The rider held up something—a cell phone?—and a beam of blue light blasted skyward.

MUZKBUX didn't like that at all. The truck swerved, jumped a curb, and barreled into a construction lot.

Straight ahead, under the glare of headlights, stood a backhoe, some covered pallets, and stacks of cement blocks.

Danny wrenched the steering wheel and yelled.

MUZKBUX slid into a large puddle of water and slammed to a stop, hurling Danny against the seat belt. A second later, all four tires burst.

The motorcycle rider had followed them. He shouted, "Get out of the truck! Get out!"

Danny didn't smell gasoline and didn't think there was any risk of explosion, but he threw himself against the door. This time it opened. He stumbled out. Mud squelched under his sneakers. His legs and arms were shaking and his breathing felt tight.

"Back off!" said the rider. He'd dismounted his motorcycle and was approaching with his cell phone in hand. He was tall and slim, wiry. His helmet had a full visor, which muffled his voice and made his face hard to see. "Cover your eyes!"

Blue light arced through the air again. Danny's ears filled with a high-pitched whine. The blue light hit MUZKBUX straight on. Purple and gold particles burst out of the truck and exploded into the air like a mushroom cloud. The force of it sent Danny

KINGS OF RUIN: ADVENTURE IN MUSIC CITY

crashing to the ground. Woozy and confused, he watched the cloud dissipate into the night air like a thousand twinkling stars.

The motorcycle rider was also thrown aside. He got to his knees and then staggered upright, gazing upward.

"Damn it!" He turned to Danny. "You okay?"

"Yeah, sure," Danny had landed hard on his left wrist, but wasn't otherwise hurt. He pulled himself up and groaned as he got a good look at MUZKBUX. He could see his future and it wasn't pretty: grounded, his allowance taken away, and just for spite, Roger might try to take his guitars, too.

All because this stupid truck had driven off on its own.

The motorcycle rider scanned the truck again. "It's safe now."

"What is that?" Danny asked. "Who are you?"

The rider tucked his phone away. "You need a ride home?"

"Do I need a ride?" Danny demanded, incredulous. "Do you know how much trouble I'm in? That stupid thing just drove off on its own. But you know why, right? You stopped it."

"Nah. I didn't do anything."

"You shot it with some crazy blue light!"

The rider climbed back onto his motorcycle. His casual tone was annoying. "Don't know what you're talking about. Sure I can't take you home?"

"Those lights," Danny said, trying to stall him. "I've seen science fiction movies. You've got some kind of special weapon. What was in the truck? An alien from outer space? Some escaped robot or something?"

The stranger laughed a little. "Too many movies rot your brain."

Danny said, "I'll tell the police all about you. Your secret hero cover or whatever will be all blown."

"You tell them whatever crazy story you want. They're just going to think you went joyriding. Come on; let me give you a ride."

Danny glared at him. "No."

"Okay." He hesitated, as if about to say something. Danny wanted it to be something helpful, something useful, something like, *Your stepdad probably won't kill you*, but then he revved the engine and rode right out of Danny's life.

Left alone, Danny's courage faltered. It was cold out and he didn't have his jacket. He didn't have his phone. He should have asked his mysterious rescuer to call the police for him, but he probably wouldn't have done it. Strangers who carried around top-secret, high-tech weapons never wanted the regular police involved, or never did in the movies.

He looked at MUZKBUX's blown tires.

Roger Rat was never going to believe him.

A few minutes later, a car approached the lot and glided to a stop. It was a late-model gray Honda Accord, nothing special, but the woman leaning out the driver's window had a familiar face.

"Mr. Kelly?" she asked. "Is that you?"

Things suddenly looked a lot brighter. "Mrs. Morris?"

She lifted her eyebrow. "What are you doing here?"

"It's a strange story," he said.

"Do you need a ride?"

"Yeah. I think I do."

Danny slid into the passenger seat. He was immediately grateful for the blast of hot air from the dashboard vent. Mrs. Morris was dressed almost like a teenager, and her hair was pulled back. He would never have guessed she was a physics teacher.

"Are you all right?" she asked. "What happened?"

"Nothing, really," Danny said.

Another arch of her eyebrow.

"I'll tell you later," he said. "Right now I'd better get home."

Danny gave her directions to his house. Mrs. Morris shifted into drive and said, as the car climbed the hill, "You're holding on to your wrist. Did you hurt it?"

"It's fine," he said. "Nothing." Eager to change the subject, he said, "You look different."

"Different better or different worse?" she asked, sounding amused.

"Better!" His face turned warm. "Not that you were ugly before."

"Beauty is only skin deep." Mrs. Morris slowed for the four-way stop sign at Fairbanks Avenue. "Like this car. Pretty enough on the outside, but inside?"

"Inside you've got a two point four liter engine, maybe two hundred horsepower at the most."

"One hundred seventy-seven," she said. "You know your cars."

"I thought I did," he admitted. "What are you doing out? Just cruising around?"

"I'm going to the football game at Waltham High," she said. "I'm looking forward to it."

Only a few moments later, she was pulling up to Roger Rat's house. Danny didn't want to leave the comfortable seat, the warmth, or Mrs. Morris. But Comet was sitting in the driveway, waiting for him patiently. The dog sat up, barked once, and wagged his tail.

"Thanks for the ride," he said.

Mrs. Morris gave him an inscrutable look. "Is there anything you want to tell me? About that truck or what happened to you tonight? I'm very trustworthy."

Danny reached for the passenger handle. "No, I'm good. Thanks for the lift."

He stood on the lawn and watched Mrs. Morris drive away.

Comet barked.

"Yeah, I know," Danny said. "The football game's on the other side of town. She was lying."

CHAPTER TEN

R uin King #5 was bored.
       During the day, it had jumped from Junior's Porsche to MUZKBUX without much excitement. After the bad man with the blue lights showed up, it leapt out of MUZKBUX into the night sky. It drifted over the sparkling lights of Piedmont, looking for a new home, and then landed in a brand new Honda Passport driven by a teenage boy named Ryan Woods.

Ryan was parked behind a movie theater, kissing a girl named Jackie Dixon.

The King liked new cars, and it liked kissing.

"I have to get home," Jackie said, pulling away. "My dad'll kill me."

Ryan kept his hands on her shoulders. "Just ten more minutes?"

She scrunched up her nose and adjusted her sweater. "He'll kill me totally dead. I've got to get home."

Ryan reluctantly turned the ignition. This was his mother's new Honda, which he'd sort of borrowed without permission for the evening. She wouldn't be happy if she found out. She wasn't going to be happy when she opened her birthday present perfume, either. All she'd wanted for her birthday was a ticket or two to Country Harvest, but they were sold out all over the place. He'd even tried talking to Danny Kelly, this kid at school whose stepdad was a bigwig music executive, and Danny had totally ignored him.

Stupid Danny Kelly.

The King hummed along with the engine strokes, happy to be surrounded by heat and motion. It tested the gas pedal a little. Pulled it down, turned the steering wheel. The Honda responded like a dream.

"Hey, what are you doing?" Jackie asked, pushing her long brown hair aside.

"Nothing!" Ryan said. "I'm not doing anything."

The King liked the sound of fear in young voices. It sped up a little more. Far ahead, it could sense another engine in motion, this one driven by a diesel engine. It formed a plan, an amazing, exciting, thrilling plan, the best it had in years. It gunned forward.

Jackie screamed, "Slow down!"

Ryan twisted the wheel, stomped on the brakes, threw the SUV into neutral.

Up ahead, warning bells and a dropping barrier.

"Stop!" Jackie yelled, but it was already too late.

CHAPTER ELEVEN

K evin couldn't believe his own stupidity.
He'd found the King just by driving around. How lucky was that? But he'd been so intent on blasting it and making sure the driver was okay (slim, dark-haired, cute driver, not that he'd noticed much) that he'd totally missed frying it.

His team was going to kill him.

He didn't want to leave that kid alone, so he'd called Mrs. Morris and asked her to pick him up. She told him that Ford and Gear had gone over to Waltham High to get readings on the parking lot, as planned.

"I'll meet them there," Kevin said.

It wasn't hard to find the high school stadium. The noise, lights, and enormous parking lot were all hard to miss. Waltham High was more blue-collar than Piedmont. Maybe it wouldn't have been so bad to go to school here. No uniforms, no snobby kids, lots of kids who worked part-time to help their families out. Kevin wouldn't have played sports, probably, but maybe they had a drama club or a band. That kid he'd saved, he looked like he'd be in the drama club.

Kevin had never had a boyfriend. He wondered what that was like, to always have someone answer when you called, someone you could count on.

Sappy sentimental stuff, he told himself.

Gear was in the south lot with Zeus on a leash. He said, "I thought you'd gone off in a big huff somewhere."

"Not a huff," Kevin protested. "Just had to clear my head."

"Is it clear now?"

Kevin wasn't quite ready to admit to losing the King. He used his own phone to scan a Chevy SUV. "Clear enough."

"You think your dad blames you about Dallas."

"I know he does."

Gear shook his head. "Maybe you two should sit down and have an actual talk about it."

"Wouldn't do any good," Kevin muttered.

As they passed three SUVS, Zeus suddenly strained forward on his leash. His nose pointed toward a blue minivan with a Piedmont sticker. He didn't bark, which was part of his training. Barking would only alert the Ruin and give it time to escape.

"Careful," Gear said.

The minivan was rocking back and forth ever so slightly, a sure sign of possession.

Kevin nodded. He activated the Focused Ruin Eradication Device—FRED—in his cell phone and aimed it at the back doors. The minivan registered 82, which was high but not as high as a King Ruin should register.

"I think we should blast it," Gear said.

Their usual policy was to isolate and eradicate. For an infestation under 75, the FRED did nice enough work and kept a vehicle clean for a year or two. For any of the King Ruins, the only thorough extermination was a full-fledged detonation of the fuel tank while the alien was trapped in the steel.

As much as he wanted to catch and destroy a King, Kevin was leery of blowing up the minivan in such a relatively public place. The Ruin was also likely to jump into any of the nearby cars, necessitating even more of a manhunt.

The minivan shifted more on its wheels. Kevin leaned forward, listening. He heard sounds a Ruin definitely wouldn't make.

Gear heard them, too. He lowered his FRED and banged his fist against the back door.

"You in there!" he said, in his best stern voice. "Come on out!"

A muffled squeak, a thud, someone's muffled voice. A tousled head rose to the window, blinked at them in surprise, and ducked down again. More thuds, a muttered curse or two, and the hatch opened. A belligerent teenage boy jumped out

"What the hell are you doing?" His hands fisted as he glared at Gear. "Who are you?"

Zeus growled.

Gear said, "Such manners."

Kevin said, "We're here to warn you. Public indecency is a misdemeanor."

The boy turned angrily. "And you're some kind of cop?"

"We're volunteers for Citizens Against Bad Morality," he said sarcastically. "We encourage abstinence, wholesome living, and better morality. You want to hear the whole sermon? It takes about forty minutes."

The girlfriend, a tall girl with long, dark hair, climbed down from the tailgate while buttoning her blouse. "Come on, Mike. Let's go back to the game."

"Yeah, Mike," Gear said. "Go on back."

The boy looked from Kevin to Gear to Zeus. He slammed the hatch shut, and with a scowl, allowed his girlfriend to pull him away toward the stadium. The girlfriend gave Kevin a backward look, obviously not thinking much of his jeans and sneakers and battered leather jacket.

Kevin waggled his fingers good-bye.

"Fag," she said with a sneer.

Zeus barked and bared his razor teeth. Which Kevin appreciated, even if he didn't care what people called him. Not at all.

When the students were gone, he and Gear scanned the minivan again. The reading had dropped to normal levels.

"That's what happens when you get a little loving going on," Gear said. Ruins got excited around love, drugs, and rock 'n' roll. No one knew why, but then again, it wasn't like you could strap one down and dissect it.

The breeze brought the smell of hot dogs to Kevin's nose. "I'm starving," he said.

"No time for food," Ford said, zigzagging his way through the cars. With him was Apollo, straining on his leash. "Something you want to report on, Kevin?"

Gear's gaze shifted to Kevin's face. He tried not to look sheepish. "I guess I kind of ran into a Ruin on the way over."

"Kind of," Ford said flatly. "Mrs. Morris just identified the driver. Daniel Kelly, a Piedmont Prep student. Did he see your face?"

"No! I'm not that dumb. I never took off my helmet."

Gear asked, "Did you fry it?"

"It jumped out," Kevin said. "I wasn't quick enough."

A cheer went up in the stadium, as if to mock him. He could feel disappointment rolling off both Gear and his dad.

Ford said, "Tell me you at least got a signature reading."

Kevin displayed the data on his phone: 5699D. Ruin King #5. Both adults sighed.

Gear said, "Well, at least we have proof it's still in town. So what now?"

Ford rubbed the side of his head. "We're going to have to cast a wider net. I told Richie Venezuela and his people to start putting out the sensor stop signs. We'll get the city's help tomorrow to work on the major intersections."

Gear asked, "Are we done here?"

"Not yet," Ford said. "I want to get more readings, see how many cars are infected."

Gear let out a low whistle. "You know the home office doesn't like big operations."

Ford said, "I'll take care of the home office."

"Good to hear." Gear tugged on Zeus's leash. "How about you two finish this lot, and I'll try the overflow lot?"

Kevin recognized what Gear was doing—leaving him with his dad to talk. As if they ever had real conversations. Once Gear was gone, they worked the rows and aisles quietly, with little chatter. Every now and then Kevin caught sight of the scoreboard: second quarter, Piedmont in the lead. Most of the students and parents were in the stands, but some knots of kids were gathered around cars with beer cans in paper bags. Kevin didn't make eye contact with them

"You saved that kid's life," Ford finally said.

Kevin tried not to think about Danny Kelly and how he might have ended up—broken neck, smashed-in skull, or incinerated in a fire. "I was just in the neighborhood."

"Still, good work," his father said. And then, a few minutes later, "Mrs. Morris said you're supposed to take the SATs next month, but now you want to cancel."

Damn. She'd ratted him out.

"I don't need them," Kevin replied. "I don't want to go to college. I don't need to for this job."

"You're not going to have this job all your life, Kevin."

"I might."

"Well, you'll never get much of a raise without a college degree."

Mrs. Morris had told him the same thing. Kevin believed them, but it wasn't as if he ever expected to be rich anyway. He didn't say that, because then he'd get the speech about ambition and realizing his true potential and all that well-meaning stuff that meant nothing at all, really.

"I don't want to sit in some stuffy classroom for the next four years," he said. "You didn't."

"Which is why we live in an RV," he said.

"Tell you what, Dad." Kevin stopped him. "Why don't we both go to college together? We can graduate in the same class. They'll let us walk the stage together and write about us in the local newspaper."

He meant it in jest, but it wouldn't be so bad, really, seeing his father on campus every day, and knowing he wasn't out putting his life in danger.

Ford's phone rang. He answered, "Yes? Where? We'll be right there."

"What is it?" Kevin asked.

"The King," Ford said grimly. "It just killed two more people."

Chapter Twelve

Fifteen minutes later, Kevin and the rest of the team were standing with other spectators at the railroad crossing on Flynn Street. Emergency lights cast red strobes against tall pine trees. Radios in squad cars squawked messages back and forth. The firemen were using saws to get to the corpses, and the cut and wrench of metal made Kevin's teeth ache.

He'd let the King escape. This was his fault.

Ford had his cell phone out. Casual observers might think he was taking pictures of the wreck, but he was instead scanning for zoron particles.

"No sign of it," Ford announced. "Let's find our guy."

Their "guy" was a middle-aged Free Mechanic named Wallace, who was standing in a parking lot nearby. He said, "I was working late, rebuilding a transmission. Heard the kid speeding down the road, heard the train gate coming down. Never something you want to listen to, you know? I rolled out and saw the whole thing."

Mrs. Morris said, rather gently, "It must have been horrible."

Wallace's gaze darted toward the flashing lights of a fire engine. "Not as bad for me as for them."

Gear tipped his head toward the office. "Can you show us what your sensors picked up?"

The garage bays smelled like grease and rubber and oil, all things Kevin found comforting. The office was a tiny, crowded alcove with one desk and a filing cabinet. The computer keyboard was dirty, but the computer itself was fairly new, thanks to the federal government. Wallace hit a few keys and they all crowded around to watch.

"This is the camera view," Wallace said. "It's mounted up on the northeast corner of the roof."

On the screen, they watched a Honda Passport SUV speed along the road toward the lowering gates of the railroad crossing. The SUV smashed through the gates, and a split second later, was broadsided by the engine of a CSX freight train. Both vehicle and train spun away from the camera's range. Kevin turned away, the back of his throat tightening up.

"The brake lights are on," Mrs. Morris observed. "The driver was trying to stop."

Ford said, "We're lucky that train was carrying produce and not chemicals. A few car derailments and this whole place would be under toxic clouds. Gear, bring up the enhanced scan."

Gear took over the keyboard and typed a few commands to activate the special software all Free Mechanics were equipped with. When the video replayed, it was with less detail but more color. The SUV showed up as bright red. A signature popped up beside it: 5699D.

Ruin King #5.

Which just confirmed what everyone had already guessed. Kevin felt sick.

"It's my fault," he said, "If I'd fried it—"

"Not your fault," Gear said. "We all know that Kings jump. They're smarter, stronger, and better at everything than other Ruins."

Mrs. Morris touched Kevin's back. "He's right."

But Ford said nothing, and he wasn't looking at Kevin.

Wallace asked, "The cops are going to want a copy of that footage, right?"

"They can have it," Gear said. He pulled out his key ring, popped off a portable storage drive, and slid it into Wallace's computer. "I'm downloading what we need. They won't even see the other data."

After they were done with Wallace's computer, the team returned to the wreckage outside. The firemen were still trying to get to the bodies. A news van had arrived, and a reporter was speaking live in front of her camera. Around her, spectators were filming the scene on their phones, probably uploading them already.

Mrs. Morris said, "There's nothing more we can do here."

"She's right," Gear said.

Ford shook his head. "We can bear witness. We can promise these victims that they didn't die in vain."

They waited and watched in the bitter night air, each of them silent.

I won't screw up next time, Kevin told himself, and hoped it was true.

Chapter Thirteen

A knock on the door woke Danny early the next morning. He had been dreaming that he and Laura were trapped in MUZKBUX as it roared down a highway, and that wasn't fun at all, but then Laura became a boy in a motorcycle helmet, tall and lean and mysterious, and they were almost kissing despite the helmet, and then—

More knocking. His mother's voice asked, "Danny? Are you awake?"

He rolled over and blinked against the harsh light of morning. "Not yet!" he said and wished she'd go away for just another hour or two.

"I need to talk to you," she said. "Now."

Comet, asleep at the end of the bed, sat up and barked.

Groaning, Danny pulled himself upright. He reached for his hooded sweatshirt and shrugged into it, mindful of the soreness in his left wrist. When he opened his door, Mom was fully dressed and had a serious expression on her face.

"The police called," she said. "Roger's truck was found near downtown with four flat tires. It was stolen out of the garage last night."

He didn't have to fake sounding groggy. "Oh."

She scrutinized him carefully. "Rachel said she and Junior left you alone last night, and the garage was closed when she got home. The keys are still in our kitchen. Anything you want to tell me?"

"Mom," he said, yawning. Behind him, his clock radio clicked on. "I just got up."

"I need you to be honest with me."

"Honest as can be." Danny held up his right hand. "I solemnly swear I did not steal your husband's truck. I'm sorry if it got trashed. It's a good-looking truck."

And that was the truth, more or less.

She stared at him for a moment longer, then sighed. "Well, Roger's very unhappy. And so am I. And I nearly tripped falling over your toy this morning. Where did you get it?"

For the first time, he noticed the cardboard box she'd brought with her. Before he could stop her, she lifted 2KEWLE from inside the box. The beach buggy looked innocent and harmless in the bright morning light.

Danny thought up a quick lie. "Eric. For my birthday."

"Don't leave it lying around," Mom said. On her way out of his room she said, "And don't be late for work."

Work. As if he was in any mood to deal with customers and condiments today. Danny took a long, hot shower while being careful of his wrist. He didn't think it was broken, but it was certainly swollen and probably sprained. He pulled on a long sleeved jersey to cover the damage and tried to decide what to do about 2KEWLE.

"What's your story, hmm?" he asked.

2KEWLE stayed perfectly silent.

Danny shoved it into his backpack. Downstairs, he ate a quick bowl of cereal and was almost away scot-free out through the garage before Roger called to him from his office.

"Hey, Dan," he said. "Come here for a minute."

Reluctantly, Danny obeyed. "I'm late for work."

"I only want to talk for a second," Roger said. He was sitting behind his desk, typing something on his laptop. The morning news played on the wall TV. Roger was dressed in crisp jeans and a cowboy shirt and wore a "Country Harvest" VIP badge around his neck.

"I heard about your truck," Danny said. "That's pretty rotten."

Roger raised his eyebrows. "Yes. Pretty rotten is one way of saying it."

Danny's sleeve had ridden up on his left wrist. He tugged it down again and shifted his backpack from one shoulder to the other. "Maybe the cops can dust it for prints. Do all that crime stuff like they do on TV."

"I'm sure they will. You were the last one in the garage. Did you hear anything? See anything?"

"No. It was pretty quiet."

"Strange how they got it out of the garage while you were asleep and before Rachel came home."

Annoyance sparked through Danny. "Is she saying I did something wrong?"

Roger's cell phone rang. He answered immediately. "Don't tell me the equipment isn't ready."

Danny shuffled impatiently. "I have to go or I'll be late."

Roger covered the phone with one hand. "This is the thing, Dan," he said. He was the only person who ever called him that, and Danny never corrected him. "A truck is just a thing, right? A collection of metal and parts. That truck, however, was given to me by my bosses for a job well done. For being cream of the crop. People get jealous of that. Sometimes they do crazy things."

Danny couldn't help himself. "You think people are jealous of you?"

Roger smiled. "Some people, yes."

"I really have to go," Danny said. "Bye."

He was relieved Roger didn't follow him. Danny grabbed his bike from the garage, hauled it out the side door through fallen leaves, and started bicycling his way downtown. He deliberately bypassed the construction lot, even though MUZKBUX had probably already been towed away.

As he pedaled, he thought about San Francisco, and how things had been so much better for him and his mom before Roger came along, how his real dad wouldn't have sat there like some condescending teacher and lectured Danny on jealousy. Jealous. Of Roger? There was nothing to be jealous about. The guy had a great house and was rich, sure, but he had lousy taste in music. He wouldn't know a good song if it kicked him in the butt.

Danny's wrist still hurt, but the farther he bicycled away from home, the more it seemed like something was wrong with his eyes, too. Or with the cars passing him in the street. Their colors were off. A silver Toyota Camry looked silver-purple with sparkles in it. A dark blue Chevy Impala looked greenish on all its edges. Danny rubbed his eyes but the weird effects didn't go away.

He was halfway to the sandwich shop when his cell phone rang.

"Did you hear?" Eric asked. "Can you believe it?"

"Hear what?" Danny asked. Surely, nothing was as exciting as what had happened to him.

Eric said, "There was a big car accident last night. Ryan Woods and his girlfriend got hit by a train. How's that for bad luck?"

CHAPTER FOURTEEN

K evin was not having a good day.
He'd barely slept at all. All he'd wanted to do was go out and find that King and fry it. Now it was morning, but he and the rest of the team were stuck listening to a teleconference briefing from the Department of Transportation. Every team deployed in the field—in Washington, Miami, and a dozen other locations—had linked in to give status reports. It was Ford's duty to report on the death of local teenagers Ryan Woods and Jackie Dixon.

No one was happy that a King had claimed more victims. Wilfred Yeomans, their boss, was especially displeased.

"What's your plan of attack, then?" he asked. The footage of the crash repeated itself in the corner of the screen, a grim and tragic loop.

Gear, hunched over the computer console with the reports he'd printed out, said, "All the data we've collected indicates this town has a high infection rate. With that many zorons to draw on, it's not likely to skip town yet."

Yeomans asked, "Are we on the verge of an Ignition?"

Zeus and Apollo stopped chewing on bones and perked up their ears.

"We don't know that yet, sir," Ford said.

An Ignition was serious business. The King would suck in the zorons from surrounding cars and become strong enough to infect a jet airplane or military drone or other deadly device.

The only logical response from headquarters was a Lightning Storm. But aerial support strikes like that required bad weather as a cover, and could only be authorized by the president of the United States.

If the president had to call a Lightning Strike on Piedmont, a lot of people were going to be very, very unhappy.

Mrs. Morris spoke up. "I think we'll know more today, sir. That King had a fresh taste of blood. If it's still around, it's likely to go after more."

"Which is precisely why you have to stop it," Yeomans said. "I expect a full report in twelve hours. And I expect good news."

The call ended.

Kevin asked, "What are we going to do, Dad?"

"We're going to mount more sensors," Ford said. "On every major intersection, real-time relay to this console. We're going to mobilize more of the Free Mechanics and get them out there doing drive-bys on their bikes and in their cars. Call them in from every county in the state if we have to. And we're going to sit on those emergency scanners. I want to know about every accident for twenty miles around, even if it's a nice old lady banging into her garbage can."

"I'll put up the sensors," Gear said.

"I'll talk to the mechanics," Mrs. Morris said.

Kevin quickly said, "I'll talk to the mechanics, too."

Ford said, "No. I want you to find out more about Daniel Kelly, that kid you saved. I want a background check on him and the truck he was driving. And you can listen to the scanners while you do the sensor calibrations."

Kevin scowled. "Why am I stuck with the calibrations?"

"Because you're the most junior, Junior," Gear said.

"And in the unlikely case you get bored, you can study for your SATs," Ford added.

They left him alone. Kevin wasn't dumb. He knew his father was punishing him for letting the King escape from Danny Kelly's truck. Ford didn't trust him anymore. Maybe none of them did.

Kevin was going to have to prove himself.

It didn't take long to run a check on Danny Kelly's truck. It had been sitting on a dealer's lot for the last three weeks, so it couldn't have brought the Ruin from Dallas. Danny himself took a little longer to investigate. Soon Kevin had copies of his birth certificate, his school records, and his PSAT scores. His picture popped up on the screen. Even cuter by day than at night. Kevin knew what music and books he liked to buy online—a lot of the same ones he liked, in fact—and it turned out that he had a part-time job here in town. Even now, he was probably making someone a turkey on rye, or maybe a whole wheat veggie with hummus.

But there was a glitch in his history. It took Kevin several minutes to find the juvenile criminal record. When he cracked it open, he found that Danny had been arrested for car theft and joyriding when he was fourteen years old. As part of the plea agreement, he couldn't get his driver's license until he was twenty-one. That probably wasn't so bad in San Francisco, where public transportation was plentiful. But then his mother had remarried and moved him to Tennessee with her and her new husband.

Kevin sat back, thinking hard.

On a hunch, he ran a check on Danny's mother and father. The mother had no history of note. The father and a younger brother, however, had been killed in a T-bone car accident that was red flagged by the Department of Transportation.

Red flag meant Ruin.

How much of a coincidence was that?

Kevin checked his watch. Lunchtime, he decided. He was in the mood for a sandwich, and Danny Kelly worked in a shop just down the street.

CHAPTER FIFTEEN

Danny pulled large covered trays of lettuce, tomato, and onions out of the refrigerator and dropped them into the sandwich prep area. He checked the oven, where long loaves of bread were steadily turning gold. The shop smelled like the chocolate chip cookies that Zinc had been baking since sun up. Zinc was on the phone, and had been for twenty minutes

"No, no," she was saying. "I heard he was a good kid. Would never go around a gate crossing."

Danny wasn't surprised that everyone in town was talking about the death of Ryan Woods and Jackie Dixon. All morning long, customers coming in for coffee, pastries, and the morning paper, had been gossiping and speculating.

"His parents are really broken up about it," Zinc said when she was done with her phone call. She was older than Danny's mom, with a streak of pink in her otherwise yellow hair. She pulled fresh hot loaves out of the oven. "You'd never try to beat a train, would you?"

"Can't drive, remember?" he said.

"Terrible thing." Zinc sighed.

Danny was trying not to think about Ryan. Maybe if he'd gotten him the Country Harvest tickets, he would have been over at one of the concerts and not out driving around on a Friday night. He reached for a tray of croissants, winced as his wrist began to throb harder, and waited until Zinc was in the back before he popped some more aspirin.

Aspirin didn't help his vision, though. Inside, everything looked fine. But whenever he looked out the window at cars, either parked or passing by, he noticed strange colors again. Not in all of them, but in enough to worry him. He wondered how he was going to explain to his mom that he needed an emergency appointment with the eye doctor.

Every now and then, he checked on his backpack, but 2KEWLE was silent and still and no trouble at all.

Business picked up steadily through the morning, and they ran out of both the cream cheese Danish and the cherry turnovers. The first lunch order of the day was from a construction worker who came in for two turkey sandwiches and a meatball sub. Danny was finishing the sandwiches when Laura came in with her friend Alice.

"Hi," Laura said, pressing up against the counter for a kiss. She was wearing a bright white sweater and her cheeks were pink from the crisp air outside. "How're things going?"

"Okay," Danny said. He pretended to like kissing her back, although the taste of lip gloss was kind of gross. "Hey, Alice."

Alice slid into one of the corner tables with an offhand wave and started messaging on her cell phone.

"Did you hear about Ryan Woods?" Laura asked. "I can't believe he got hit by a train like that. It's crazy. He always followed the rules, you know?"

Zinc came over. "Danny, are you done with these orders?"

Danny rang up the order for the construction worker. Then he and Zinc had to tend to a sudden rush of students and parents from the karate dojo that was just a few doors away in the strip mall. Laura retreated to the booth with Alice. As he worked, he was aware of Laura watching him and occasionally giggling.

"Young love," Zinc said. "I had me a bad case of that once."

Danny stayed quiet.

At noon, just as Danny was beginning to lose track of orders, Zinc's twenty-year-old nephew Gary showed up to help out. Gary was six-foot-three, had long hair to his waist, and spent most of his days playing video games. "Dude, you're working slow today," he said as Danny made a sandwich. "What's wrong with your wrist?"

"Nothing." Danny pulled his sleeve down. "Played too much guitar last night."

Gary wrinkled his nose, skeptical, but didn't argue over it.

The crowd slowed and things got a little easier. Danny was thinking of taking a break to go talk to Laura when a tall teen with shaggy blond hair came in. He was Danny's age or maybe a little older, but not by much. He was wearing a black leather jacket.

Danny had a definite weakness for black leather jackets.

"What can I get you?" Danny asked.

The kid scanned the overhead board quickly. "Two roast beef on wheat, American cheese, mustard, and tomato."

Danny pulled on new plastic gloves and started making the order. Under the jacket, the kid was wearing a white T-shirt that read "FOREVER 27." Danny bet most people didn't know what the slogan meant.

"Brian Jones," he said.

The kid gave him an appraising look. "Blind Owl Wilson."

"Jimi Hendrix."

Gary squinted at the two of them. "What are you two talking about?"

"Janice Joplin," the kid replied.

Danny said, "Club Twenty-seven is a bunch of famous musicians or singers who died when they were twenty-seven years old. Starting with Brian Jones, one of the founders of The Rolling Stones. Including Kurt Cobain and Jim Morrison."

"Never heard of them," Gary said.

Danny dismissed him and focused on the stranger. "Not from around here, are you?"

"Nevada. You?"

"California."

So they were two Westerners stranded in Hicksville. Danny reached for the mustard and squeezed out a generous amount. "Moving here?" he asked, trying to sound casual about it.

"Passing through."

Laura must have been watching them. She came up to the counter and asked sweetly, "So, Danny, change your mind about tomorrow?"

"Tomorrow?" Danny asked blankly.

"Country Harvest. You don't have to like the singers, you know. There's a fairway and rides and lots of free stuff the record companies give away."

The stranger arched an eyebrow. Danny could practically hear him thinking *Country Harvest?*

"No," Danny said to Laura. "I still have to work."

Laura gave a little pout. "But it's your birthday. Maybe you could get off early."

Danny started to wrap up the sandwiches. "You want a pickle with these?"

The stranger asked, "Just one?"

"One each," he said. "Free. Kosher."

"Well, if they're kosher." He appeared to be pondering the momentous decision. "Sure. Only because it's your birthday tomorrow."

Danny had the distinct impression the stranger was flirting with him. Which was such a novel experience that he almost sliced his finger open on a cutting knife. He didn't like it—no, he couldn't, because he had a cover to maintain—but then again, it was kind of nice, and he *did* look good in that leather jacket.

Laura turned and snapped, "What does kosher have to do with his birthday?"

"Wow," Gary said from behind Danny. "Catfight!"

Danny quickly moved to the register and rang up the order.

"You're not from around here," Laura said to the kid. "You should go back to wherever."

"Thanks for the advice," he said dryly.

Laura looked to Danny, but he didn't know what to say. She said, "Fine. Don't come if you don't want to, Danny."

She turned on her heel and stormed out, her leather boots clicking as she went. Alice, startled, had to hurry out of the booth to catch up with her. Danny was confused. How was this his fault? But he didn't try to go after her.

"Girlfriend?" the kid asked.

"Sort of," Danny said. "That'll be nine dollars."

He handed over a twenty-dollar bill. "What's Country Harvest?"

"It's a music concert," Danny said.

Zinc, who was slicing cheese, said, "Don't play it down. Big time stars get together at the fairgrounds all weekend, all to benefit charity. It started yesterday. There's going to be fifteen, twenty thousand people there."

"All country music," Danny said.

Zinc laughed. "Don't say it like it's a disease, hon."

The kid's phone rang. He turned to answer it, shielding it from view, but Danny caught a glimpse anyway: large and square and ugly.

"Keep the change," the kid said hurriedly, and left before Danny could say anything.

He knew that phone. It was the same kind the mysterious motorcycle rider had used to zap MUZKBUX.

CHAPTER SIXTEEN

I've got to go talk to that guy," Danny said to Gary and Zinc. He pulled off his apron and shoved it into the corner. "I'll be right back."

He hurried out of the sandwich shop. The cool afternoon air cut through his shirt as he scanned the cars in the parking lot. But the stranger was on foot, not in a car. He was crossing the far corner of the lot and heading toward another bunch of shops in Piedmont's bustling downtown area.

Shivering, Danny went back inside. Gary was filling the sweet tea thermos, and Zinc was wiping down the booth where Alice and Laura had been sitting.

Zinc gave him an appraising look. "Why'd you lie about working tomorrow?"

He wished she hadn't heard that. "It's no big deal."

"It's a big deal when you lie, Danny," she said. "Especially with that girl, who's never done you wrong. If you're interested in someone else, that's one thing. But don't make up excuses. You tell her to her face."

From the counter, Gary said, "Tell that to my last girlfriend. She broke up with me by sending me a text message."

"I wasn't talking to you," Zinc said.

"I'll tell her the truth," Danny promised. "Can I take my lunch break now? I'll be back in a half hour."

"Okay, but don't be late. We've got a lot of work to do."

He grabbed his jacket, and on second thought, grabbed his backpack as well. Quickly, he bicycled after Kevin, who was turning down a side street. The street dead-ended into a junkyard fronted by a two-story brick garage. Stacked around the garage was a sprawling maze of broken, abandoned cars. Danny thought it was kind of sad, all those cars that had once been cared for, but now left to rot and rust under the sun or snow.

There, for instance. A solid black Ford Buick, twenty years or so old, smashed up so badly that its front end looked like large metal spaghetti. Behind it was a green Chevy Cavalier that looked almost drivable, except all the doors had been torn off. *Every car has a story*, he thought. That sounded like the start of a song. He told himself to remember it later.

Unlike most other cars he'd seen that morning, the black Buick really was black and the green Chevy really was green. In fact, almost all the cars in the junkyard were the colors they were supposed to be. Whatever was wrong with his eyes, it wasn't wrong right now.

He didn't see where Kevin had gone, so he parked his bike and found an office inside the garage. It was a rat's hole of filing cabinets and boxes. The air smelled like grease. If he dropped a match, the whole place might explode into a raging inferno. A thin man was sitting behind a desk, an unlit cigarette jammed between his lips. The sign on his desk said "Richie Venezuela, Manager."

"What do you want?" Venezuela said.

Not very polite, Danny decided. But he was from the big city. He could handle rude.

"A guy came over to Zinc's Sandwiches, forgot his change," he said. "I brought it for him."

"There's no guy here."

"He walked right here," Danny said. "My age, blond hair."

Venezuela shrugged. "You see him anywhere?"

"He left without his change."

"How much change?"

Danny thought fast. "Ten bucks."

"Well, leave it here. If anyone shows up, I'll give it to him."

"Never mind," Danny said.

He stepped out into the bright, crisp air, glad to be out of the greasy-smelling air. He didn't think the guy would appreciate it if he started exploring the junkyard on his own, but he really wanted to see Kevin again. He reached for his bicycle handlebars and heard a distinctive whirring sound.

2KEWLE bumped and rolled in his backpack. His tiny horn sounded.

Danny slung the backpack off and opened the zipper. 2KEWLE rolled out, looking disgruntled. He rolled back and forth, flashed his headlights, and steered himself around the corner of the building.

"Wait up," Danny said.

2KEWLE navigated his way through twenty feet of metal maze before stopping. Danny peered around a stack of used tires and saw a thirty-foot long RV parked by the back fence. It was battered and worn on the outside, but in his skewed vision, it shone bright white, almost too bright to look at.

"What is that?" he asked.

2KEWLE made a soft mewling sound, like a kitten, and backed away. Danny got the distinct impression the buggy didn't want to get too close to the RV.

"You think he went there?"

2KEWLE stayed silent.

"You are a strange little toy," Danny said. He scooped 2KEWLE up and eased him back into his backpack. "Time to find out more about you, buddy."

CHAPTER SEVENTEEN

Eric's house was a big mansion with more rooms than Danny could count. In the basement was a finished entertainment room full of toys, board games, a pool table, a big screen TV, and a bar stocked with snacks and soda. Eric chewed on a granola bar as he eyed 2KEWLE, who sat on the game table looking forlorn and dirty.

"So it's remote-controlled," Eric said. "What's the big deal?"

"I need to find out who's controlling it," Danny said. He checked his watch. He'd bicycled over with 2KEWLE under his arm, and only had fifteen minutes before he had to get back to the sandwich shop.

Eric's annoying younger sister, Emily, looked up from the game she was playing on the TV. "It's not remote-controlled."

"Shut up, squirt." Eric turned 2KEWLE over. "Where's the on/off switch?"

"I don't know," Eric said.

Emily piped up again. "On the controller."

Eric said, "Don't make me come over there and tickle you."

"Like you could catch me," Emily scoffed.

"What controller?" Danny asked her.

She left the game control on the rug and climbed up on a stool. She was only ten and short for her age.

"It's not a remote control because 'remote' means there'd be a wire connecting it to a controller, and there's obviously no wire." Emily picked up 2KEWLE and turned it over. "This one's r/c—radio controlled. There's a receiver inside. And a transmitter, too."

Eric leaned over and messed up Emily's hair. "Ain't she smart? That's why we keep her."

"Quit it," Emily said, squirming out from under Eric's hand.

She peered at the underside some more. "Looks like someone bought the chassis and built on it from there. See in there? That's a custom-made circuit board. Someone spent a lot of money."

"How come you know so much?" Danny asked.

Eric said, "She's got her own helicopter fleet."

"It's not a *fleet*." Emily slipped off the stool and padded in her bare feet to a cabinet built into the wall. The doors swung open with a click. Inside sat a half dozen tiny helicopters carefully arranged on the shelves.

"That's an Ocean Rescue," she said, pointing. "That's an Apache, and that's a Hughes—"

Eric interrupted her. "My little sister is really a boy on the inside."

"Shut up," Emily said.

Danny turned his attention back to 2KEWLE. "From how far away can someone control them? A mile or two?"

Emily folded her arms. "I'm not going to tell you because my brother is a big jerk."

Eric barreled around the table to chase her down the length of the entertainment room. "We'll see who's a jerk, squirt!"

Danny ignored the two of them and studied 2KEWLE some more. "How fast does it go?"

"I'm not telling you!" Emily yelled, just as Eric caught her in a big bear hug.

"You guys have been a lot of help." He wrapped 2KEWLE up in his jacket again and headed for the basement door. "I've got to get back to work."

He left the two of them squabbling and got on his bicycle. Most of the trip back to Zinc's was downhill, which made the going easy. At the corner of Clemson and Colgate, he slowed to watch a black man who was erecting a portable stop sign. The man was dressed in civilian clothes and had a yellow city truck. After the man got the sign fixed in place, he pulled out his cell phone, as if answering a call.

A very big cell phone, in fact.

Then he swung it in an arc, and 2KEWLE went wild in Danny's backpack.

"Hey!" Danny shouted, as 2KEWLE slammed and bucked against his back. He dropped the backpack on the pavement and the zipper split open. 2KEWLE rolled out. Part of his rear fender was hanging loose, damaged in the fall. He raced away with the fender dragging on the road.

"No, wait!" Danny called.

The man in the city worker uniform shouted, "You there! Stop that toy!"

Danny bicycled fast after 2KEWLE, and the man chased after them both.

Chapter Eighteen

D anny wasn't much of a runner, but he wanted to catch 2KEWLE before the stranger did. He heard the city truck rev up behind him but didn't dare look back.

Colgate Avenue was a tree-lined lane of mansions, garages, and guest houses. The trees were turning red with autumn, and the big, broad lawns were littered with fallen leaves. 2KEWLE abruptly turned into a wide driveway, plowed through a pile of maple and oak leaves, and barreled up a path into someone's backyard. Danny biked past a discarded rake and chased 2KEWLE toward a white gazebo.

"You, kid!" a gardener yelled. "What are you doing?"

2KEWLE showed no signs of slowing down as it barreled down a hillside toward someone else's backyard. Danny had to abandon his bicycle and scramble through brush in order to follow. He wondered how many trespassing laws he was breaking for the sake of a little toy buggy.

When he was free of the brush, he found himself in the middle of a large lawn with its own brick terrace and covered swimming pool. The white house in front of him was three stories tall and looked almost as big as Eric's. 2KEWLE was halfway toward the garage and showed no signs of slowing down.

"Come back!" Danny yelled.

From behind a large wooden fence came the sound of the yellow truck.

Danny ran as fast as he could toward the garage. He was within fifty feet when a barking German shepherd streaked out from around the corner and leapt toward him. The dog was huge, with enormous sharp teeth. Danny hurled himself backward with only a moment to spare.

He expected to land hard, but instead hit a sheet of thick plastic.

The pool cover broke free, trapping him. The cold water of the swimming pool closed in over Danny's head.

❖

The funny thing about drowning was that Danny didn't feel like he was drowning at all. On some dim level, he was aware of cold water in his mouth and nose and ears, and of not being able to breathe past the big cement block in his lungs. But he didn't feel afraid, either. He felt sleepy and calm and ready for whatever came next.

What came next wasn't his life flashing before him, but two specific memories instead. In the first, he was sitting in their house back in San Francisco, watching TV in the living room. He was eight years old. It was rainy outside the windows, but inside all was warm and bright. Dad was due home any minute now, he and Mickey both. The house smelled like Mom's meatloaf, and the table was set for four.

In his memory, he couldn't remember what exact TV show he'd been watching, but it was some kind of documentary. Big black birds swept in and grabbed mice, rabbits, and other things hopping around on a prairie. The footage both fascinated and appalled him. Birds eating mice, yuck. He barely heard the phone ring. His mother answered, but then she was silent, just listening, and something about that made Danny get off the rug where he was sitting and go around the corner to the kitchen.

His mother was standing with her back to the sink. One hand held the phone to her ear, and her other hand was pressed to her chest as if something hurt. Her mouth was open just a little bit. Her eyes were staring right at Danny, but he didn't think she actually saw him.

The unnatural stillness of her posture and the dazed expression on her face made Danny shrink back, but it was too late. He had already seen something horrible sweeping in on their lives like an enormous black bird with razor sharp talons. He just hadn't felt the pain himself yet, and wouldn't until Mom sat down and told him exactly what had happened.

The second memory that flashed through Danny as he was drowning also took place in that kitchen in San Francisco. Years had passed; he'd grown taller, stronger. The curtains were different. The furniture had been replaced. But Mom was the same, just a little older and shorter from his perspective. She had a job working in marketing and advertising. They were a team. She kept them housed, fed, and clothed. He went to school and played his guitar and tried to stay out of trouble, though there had been a very bad time right before Christmas when he'd gotten into enough trouble for his entire lifetime. On this night, she had made his favorite dinner, spaghetti and meatballs. The wind was hard against the windows, but inside it was warm, and the air smelled like garlic.

"I have news," Mom said. She looked excited and worried at the same time, which made Danny nervous.

"News I'm going to like?" he asked.

She sat down. "News that I like. Roger and I are going to get married."

Roger was some guy she'd been dating once in a while, whenever business brought him to town. Danny had met him at dinner once. Some fancy restaurant that required jackets for the men, and where the waiters expected you to know what foie gras was. Like Danny cared anything about snobbery like that. Roger was okay enough for Mom to date, though he had a narrow face and little eyes that reminded Danny of a rat.

"Danny?" Mom asked. "Did you hear me?"

He poked at his spaghetti. "Roger lives in the middle of nowhere."

"Nashville is not the middle of nowhere. You're going to like it there."

Which was when he'd seen the bird again—that big black bird swooping down out of the sky to grab at him and rip him open with its talons. The bird was back except now it was plastic and cold and dragging him down into a watery grave—

Suddenly, he coughed. Water tore out of his chest and up his throat, flooding through his mouth and out to the concrete pool deck below his cheek. The black man was bent over him, breathing hard.

"You scared the crap out of me, kid," he said.

More water choked out of Danny in a vicious spasm. The cold, slimy liquid burned his nose, and he retched helplessly.

"Come on," the man said, just as the world turned dark. The last thing Danny heard was: "You're coming with me."

CHAPTER NINETEEN

K evin was sitting in the Pit, calibrating the sensors his father and Gear were setting out in different parts of the city. They had gone to the city's public works department, flashed their official badges, and borrowed a city truck to get the job done. The zoron sensors would be mounted on stop signs, traffic lights, and telephone poles. Tiny but very powerful, they would spread a surveillance net that would locate and track Ruin #5.

"Sensor twelve mounted," Ford said.

"Got it," Kevin replied over his headset.

"Where's Gear?"

"Went offline a few minutes ago," Kevin said.

"Anything else happening?"

Kevin thought about the sandwich shop. He hadn't learned anything new by checking up on Danny Kelly, but it had been kind of nice seeing him again. In a totally not-romantic, not-attracted-to-him kind of way, because Kevin didn't do attachments.

Still, if he were going to have a fantasy boyfriend, that boyfriend would totally look like Danny Kelly.

"Nothing else is going on," he told his dad.

Ten minutes later, Gear showed up with a totally drenched Danny by his side. Danny was coughing and shivering and looked like a drowned rat. Gear didn't look much better.

"What the—" Kevin asked, startled. "You can't bring him here!"

"Kid nearly drowned," Gear said. "Get a blanket."

Gear lowered Danny to the sofa. Kevin grabbed several blankets and towels from a cabinet and dropped them over him. Danny caught his gaze and started to say something like, "You—" but then hacked up more water and couldn't finish the sentence.

"Make some coffee," Gear said.

Kevin put water on to boil. He closed the computer console doors, hoping to hide their equipment, but it was obvious Danny had already seen them. He only hoped Danny wouldn't mention the sandwich shop. He didn't think Ford or Gear would approve of that little field trip.

"Who are you people?" Danny asked. "Spies?"

Gear was already calling Ford, asking him to return. Kevin said, "No, not spies," but didn't know how much he really could tell him.

Danny pulled the blankets tighter and tilted his head. "You were the one last night, right? You zapped my stepdad's truck."

"Me?" Kevin asked.

"You're built like he was. Tall. And you have the same phone."

Kevin busied himself making coffee and hot chocolate and didn't answer. Danny huddled into the blankets and looked around, taking everything in. Not that there was much to see— battered furniture, an old TV, some magazines. Ford arrived a few minutes later and looked very unhappy to see they had a guest.

Ford said to Gear, "Tell me everything."

"The kid's got a radio-controlled buggy that scored a ninety-two," Gear said. "I couldn't get a signature reading before it bolted. I chased them both, and this one fell into a pool. The buggy got away."

"What's a ninety-two?" Danny asked.

"A buggy?" Kevin asked. "Like a toy?"

Danny sneezed. "What are we talking about here? Aliens? Ghosts? Robots from another dimension?"

Kevin said, "Again with the science fiction movies."

Danny's gaze met his in that moment, and Kevin felt it. A glint. A glimmer. Some kind of connection between them. It was warm and interesting, and Kevin wanted more of it.

Ford interrupted their moment. "It doesn't matter what exactly they are. The important thing is that we stop them."

Danny sneezed again. "Are they what's making all the cars look funky?"

Kevin was so surprised he almost dropped his hot chocolate. Gear and Ford exchanged looks and Ford asked, "Funky?"

Danny wilted a little. "Never mind. It's nothing."

But it wasn't nothing, Kevin knew. It was hugely important. He leaned forward and asked, "What do you see when you look at cars?"

"I don't even know your names," Danny said.

"I'm Kevin," Kevin said. "That's Ford and that's Gear. Nice to meet you."

Again, with that connection, that glint. Danny's shoulders relaxed a little. "Yeah. I guess."

Ford leaned forward. "Listen to me. Did you hear about that car that got hit by a train last night? The kids who got killed?"

Danny nodded. "They went to my school."

"These things we're chasing, they kill people," Ford said. "And they'll kill more people. It's very rare, but not unknown, that people who have been exposed to them develop the ability to see them. You were exposed last night to the one in your stepdad's truck. The effect usually wears off in a few days, but if you can see them now, just by looking at a car, that'll help us a lot."

Danny looked to Kevin for confirmation. Kevin nodded, strangely proud that Danny seemed to trust him.

"I see colors," Danny admitted. "Yellow and greens, some orange. Like it's the car's real color under the paint job. This RV?

Bright white, though you obviously haven't cleaned the outside in a few years."

"Bright white means a vehicle's been zapped," Gear said. "The more purple you see, the more infested a car is. If we drive him around town, he might be able to see the King just by looking at it."

"What's a King?" Danny asked.

Kevin didn't like it. Number one, driving Danny around and hoping to see the King was like combing a haystack for a needle. Number two, Danny was a civilian. He didn't have any training or background in dealing with Ruins.

"Maybe we could handle it ourselves," Kevin said to his father.

But Ford was looking intently at Danny. "Don't you want to help, Danny?"

Danny sneezed again. "Yeah, sure. But I'm supposed to be at work right now. Zinc's going to kill me for taking off like that. And my cell phone's all waterlogged. My mom will freak if she can't reach me."

"We'll take care of all that," Ford said. "Kevin, take him home to get some dry clothes. Then drive him around and see what you can find."

Kevin didn't like it. "But he doesn't even have a security clearance!"

"I'll take care of that," Ford said.

CHAPTER TWENTY

Ford made Danny sign a bunch of papers that said, basically, he was about to learn a bunch of national security secrets. If he told anyone, he could end up in prison for the rest of his life. It was pretty serious stuff, but Danny couldn't stop sneezing, and he was distracted by the smell of slimy pool water that had soaked into his clothes. Afterward, Kevin drove him home in a Mazda that gave off a horrible screech when it first started.

"Your fan belt's slipping," Danny said, muffled from the blankets he still had wrapped around him.

"No kidding," Kevin replied. "Are your parents going to be at home?"

"No. They're at the music festival. It's their job."

Kevin fell silent. Danny wanted to ask him a dozen questions, beginning with all that high-tech equipment in the RV and how Kevin had gotten into this crazy line of work. But he felt a little awkward, too, because Kevin was ridiculously good-looking, and whenever Danny looked at him, he felt in danger of abandoning his heterosexual cover forever.

"How old are you?" Danny asked.

"Seventeen."

"And this is what you do? Drive around and try to catch these things?"

SAM CAMERON

"More or less."

Kevin didn't sound happy to have Danny riding along. Which was too bad, because it hadn't been Danny's idea to nearly drown in a pool or get caught up in some kind of top secret government operation.

On the other hand, it was kind of cool, too.

When they reached Danny's house, they found Rachel sitting at the kitchen island and painting her fingernails bright red. She asked, "What happened to you?"

"Went swimming," Danny said.

"Who are you?" Rachel asked, sizing up Kevin.

He didn't flinch under the scrutiny. "I'm new in town."

"Since when?" Rachel asked.

"Doesn't matter." Danny started trudging up the stairs. "I'll be down in a few minutes."

He was nervous about what Kevin and Rachel could talk about while he was upstairs, but he was going to go crazy if he didn't get the slimy smell off his skin. He took a short, hot shower and swallowed two aspirin against the pain in his wrist. When he emerged from the bathroom in only a towel, he was mortified to see Kevin sitting on his bed, reading one of his music magazines.

"Hey!" he said. "A little privacy!"

Kevin didn't look up from the pages. "I'm not looking. Your stepsister wanted to ask me all sorts of questions so I had to escape."

"She's okay."

"She thinks I'm your secret boyfriend."

Danny felt his face turn bright red. "She does not. She doesn't know—I mean, no one knows. I'm not."

Kevin's expression turned thoughtful. "You aren't?"

"Not officially," Danny said.

"Unofficially?"

"Not at all," Danny replied firmly. "She was just messing with you. I'm not, you know. Gay."

Kevin's eyebrows went up. "You're sure about that?"

Danny grabbed clothes out of his closet and went back to the bathroom. His chest felt tight and his heartbeat too quick. Maybe he was having a panic attack. He'd never had one before, but now seemed like a good time to start. If Rachel thought he was gay then other kids did too, probably, Junior and all the rest, and all of Danny's careful hard work was for nothing.

He stared in the mirror. What did Rachel see when she looked at him? What did Kevin see? Danny messed up his hair, then combed it back, then deliberately didn't put on any deodorant, then decided he didn't want to smell bad all day.

When he came out again, Kevin was looking at the framed pictures on his desk. Most were of friends and family back in San Francisco. One of the photos was of Danny, his dad, and his brother before their car accident.

"They died in a wreck when I was little," Danny said.

Kevin's voice was quiet. "My mom did, too."

Danny cleared his throat. "About the other thing—"

"No problem," Kevin said. "You're not gay."

"Are you?" Danny blurted out.

"Yeah." Kevin didn't sound worried or eager about it, just routine. He reached into his pocket. "Here, take this. Courtesy of the U.S. government until yours dries out."

It was a cell phone, nice enough but not the high-tech kind that Kevin carried. Danny turned it on and checked the signal. "So now what? We just drive around?"

"Not so much," Kevin said.

Fifteen minutes later, they were parked downtown near the town library. The sun was shining down on the afternoon traffic and the library's Halloween decorations. Kevin propped a silver box up against the steering wheel and started scanning cars as they passed.

"Let's test this ability of yours," he said. "What color is that Lincoln Town Car?"

Danny squinted. "Bluish-green."

"It's scoring a twenty-two," Kevin said. "These things we're tracking radiate signatures and strengths. If a car has a twenty-two, it's not a lot to worry about. Maybe the engine light goes on every once in a while for no good reason, or the headlights flicker now and then."

"Gear said 2KEWLE was a ninety-two."

"2KEWLE?"

"The buggy."

Kevin hesitated. "Yes. That's got to be wrong, though."

"Why?"

"Because these things only affect combustible fuel engines. They look for things with gas and spark plugs. A remote-controlled toy doesn't have either."

"If these things are in people's cars, how come the government doesn't send out a warning? Zap everybody's cars and clean them out?"

Kevin kept his eyes on the traffic. "In biology class, did they tell you about the million kinds of bacteria in your gut?"

"The what?" Danny asked.

"Your intestines. You've got all this bacteria in there, right? Everyone does. Like, two or three pounds of a million different kinds. And most of the time you don't even notice. It's like that with the Ruins."

Danny asked, "That's what you call them? Ruins?"

Kevin said, "Yeah. The important thing is they're only a problem once in a while. You could have one in your car all your life and never notice. They're made of these tiny particles, and the more they have, the stronger and more mischievous they get. The bigger they get, the more trouble they cause. The really big ones are called Kings. They're the ones you have to watch out for."

Danny thought of 2KEWLE. Sure, he might have scored a 92, but he didn't seem like he was going to start going around killing people.

"Are they smart?" he asked.

"No. How about that Ford Focus over there?"

"Looks kind of green to me." Danny shifted uncomfortably in his seat, which had a broken-down spring somewhere deep inside. "And so you and your friends go around wiping these things out?"

"Yes. What about that pickup truck?"

Danny glanced at the Ford F-150. "It's a yellow."

Kevin consulted his phone. "Yellow is a sixty. Think of the visible light spectrum. Purple is the short wave end, red is the long wave, and yellow is the middle."

"If that guy's car is going to try to kill him, we should tell him!"

"A forty-five won't kill you. You just spend a lot of time in the shop because they break down a lot."

"So the Ruin, whatever, is stuck in the car and can't leave?"

Kevin hesitated.

"Come on," Danny said. "I signed those papers."

Reluctantly, he said, "Normal Ruins just sort of stick on a car like gum on your shoe. Only the strong ones—the Kings— can move around freely. A King can jump to another car or up in the air, and land a mile or two away."

"How many Kings are there?"

"Around here? Just one."

"Have you run into this one before?"

A red van passed, registering 15. Kevin said, "It's hard to say," and then turned his gaze squarely to Danny. "Why not gay?"

"What?"

"Why aren't you gay?" Kevin asked.

Danny tried not to get defensive about it. "Why would I be? People think they can tell stuff by looking at you, but that doesn't make it true."

Kevin's gaze didn't waver. "So you kiss your girlfriend, maybe pet her, or whatever, and you like it?"

Danny looked away. "It's not like that."

"It's girls or boys," Kevin replied. "Or both if you're bisexual."

"I'm not bisexual," Danny said, hating that Kevin was trying to make him say it, admit it, when it was really none of his business.

A gray Honda Accord pulled into the space beside them. Danny watched Mrs. Morris slide out from behind the wheel carrying a bag. She was dressed today in slim black slacks and a green blouse that set off her beautiful eyes. She leaned against his door and handed the bag to Kevin.

"I brought you two crazy kids some chocolate milkshakes," she said.

"You're a lifesaver," Kevin said.

Mrs. Morris's full wattage smile turned on Danny. "Nice to see you again. I hear you're in on all our secrets."

"Not all of them," Kevin said. "Limited secret clearance."

She smiled even wider, as if security laws were only guidelines. "How goes the hunting?"

"Lots of colors but no purples," Kevin said.

"It's a big town," Mrs. Morris said. "Cars zooming up and down the highway, all the back roads, in and out of shopping malls, in and out of garages. Very hard to locate on the street level."

"I could go up in a helicopter," Danny suggested.

"I doubt your special ability works more than thirty or forty feet away," Mrs. Morris said. "Let's try it."

They left the cars and climbed up the grassy slope behind the library. Danny liked walking behind Kevin and looking at his long legs. Well, his legs and his butt and the way his jacket hung off his shoulders, all of him. At the top of the hill, he was disappointed to discover that all the cars on the street looked normal.

"I thought so." Mrs. Morris shivered a little in the brisk wind. "I've never read of a case where it worked from a great distance. Still, it was worth a try."

Danny gazed out over Piedmont. He hadn't thought much of the town, not after the hills and excitement of San Francisco, but that was different now that he knew there were things out there that could kill people. He looked at all the little cars, all the drivers who knew nothing. He thought about Ryan Woods and Jackie Dixon and how it must have been for them, hurtling toward the oncoming train and knowing they were going to die.

"People should know that they're in danger," he said.

"You're in danger every day you walk this earth," Mrs. Morris said calmly.

Kevin dug his hands deeper into his jacket. "I'd want to know."

Danny almost said, *I want to know, too.* He wanted to know what it was like to kiss a boy so hard his toes curled, and slide hard together on a bed, and do all the things that so far had only happened in his fantasies. Kevin probably had done all those things and more. After all, he was seventeen. But he had the luxury of not living in Piedmont, and not having to live with Roger Rat, and not going to high school every day with well-dressed rednecks.

The wind picked up even more and they went back down the slope. Back in the parking lot, Danny's sparkly vision still didn't return. "Your cars aren't white anymore," he said.

Kevin and Mrs. Morris looked at each other and then at him.

"What about that BMW?" Kevin said, pointing at the intersection.

He squinted as hard as he could. The silver BMW 1 series remained silver. The blue Chevy Cavalier behind it stayed blue.

Mrs. Morris said, "It seems as though your ability has worn off."

"No," Danny said. "It can't. Ford said it lasts a few days!"

"Not for you," Kevin said, sounding disappointed. But nowhere near as disappointed as Danny was.

CHAPTER TWENTY ONE

Officer Jennifer McCoy of the Piedmont Police Department came on duty Saturday afternoon at three o'clock. Everyone at the precinct was talking about those two teenagers killed at the train crossing. Such a shame, they said. Most cops couldn't afford tuition at Piedmont Prep and didn't know Ryan or Jackie, but it was a tragedy for any teenager to die so senselessly.

"Did he try to get around the gate?" McCoy asked her boss, Sergeant Ross.

Ross shook his head. "There was footage from a garage just up the street. Looks like the brakes weren't working."

McCoy checked out her gear and attended the afternoon briefing. A lot of tourists were in town for the Country Harvest musical fair. It was just her bad luck to be scheduled to work until midnight. Lots of visitors meant lots of traffic control and the increased risk of drunk drivers. Good chance of overtime pay, though. After the briefing, McCoy went down to the garage and got her assigned patrol vehicle, number twelve, which was a six-year-old Crown Victoria that smelled like old cheeseburgers.

She didn't know that it had last been used on the night shift.

In fact, patrol car number twelve had been first on the scene to the train crash tragedy. The officer driving it had been too busy with the wreck to notice the blue lights seeping out of the woods and into his vehicle.

King #5 had found himself a new home.

The King liked police cars, even when they weren't brand-new. He especially liked the sirens and warning lights. He felt Officer McCoy's weight settle into the seat and waited a few minutes for the engine to warm up before he turned the siren on. The bright, sharp wail made him happy. Officer McCoy slapped at the switch quickly and he shut it off, but only for a moment. The next blast made him even happier. She slapped again, cursed. He liked it when drivers grew frustrated with him.

Better not to spoil all the fun too quickly, though. The King shut the siren down. He could sense Officer McCoy's confusion and relief. For a few minutes, he was inactive while they cruised around downtown Piedmont. He saw it only in terms of steel and engines, flesh and non-flesh. His kind were frequent. Small but common, some of them growing bigger, but never as big as he was.

He turned on the strobe lights. Flicked on the siren.

"What's going on?" McCoy demanded. "Stupid car."

They always blamed the car, never seeing beyond steel to him. Never sensing that he was the one in charge.

He didn't want to be returned to the garage and didn't feel like jumping yet. Instead, he quieted down. Bided his time. When McCoy pulled over a speeder and got out of him to investigate, he followed an inch or two. Then an inch or two more. He liked the gold-colored Volvo in front of him, even if it was too old for his tastes.

He nudged up against the Volvo's bumper, then eased back again.

But when McCoy got back behind the wheel, he decided to have some real fun.

CHAPTER TWENTY-TWO

"I'll take you home, Danny," Mrs. Morris said. "I'm on my way that way now."

"But I want to help," Danny protested. He looked at Kevin. "Even if I can't see anything special, I'm not useless."

Kevin wanted Danny to stay. It was nice to have someone his own age to talk to about this stuff, after all. And even though Danny said he wasn't officially gay—a total lie Kevin could totally see through—there was no denying that physical attraction, either.

On the other hand, civilians could get hurt in this job. And Kevin was already responsible for two deaths in this town.

"You should go look for your buggy," he said. "If it turns up, call us. I put the numbers in the phone I gave you."

Danny went with Mrs. Morris reluctantly.

Kevin stayed with the Mazda and continued to monitor traffic. It was lonely without someone in the passenger seat. Dusk came, the people of Piedmont closing their businesses and going home. A Volvo C70 ran a red light, only to be pulled over by a police cruiser. The female officer got out to write the ticket. The Volvo driver, a bald man wearing sunglasses, started to argue.

The patrol car rolled forward a little, all on its own.

Kevin's phone rang. Ford was on the other end, asking if Danny found anything at all.

"No," he replied, scanning the police car. "But I think I did."

100 points.

Bingo.

"It's here, on Main Street, in a police car," he said. "Right in front of me."

"Stay right where you are!" Ford ordered. "I'll be right there."

Kevin promised he would, but just a moment or two later, the police officer climbed back in her car and started off again with lights and sirens. Kevin had no choice but to follow. He was careful in his driving but kept up as the police car cut across the road, turned down the length of Mill Road, and blasted through an intersection at Wells and Fourth.

Kevin called his dad back. "I'm following her, but I don't think she's responding to a call. There's nothing on the police scanner."

"We're tracking you," Ford said. "Don't try and take this King on your own!"

The police car sped up. It cornered onto Miller's Bridge so fast it almost rose up on two wheels. The two-lane bridge crossed thirty feet above the Cumberland River, which was fast moving and treacherous after all the summer rain. With sirens blaring and lights swirling, the car made it halfway across the bridge, crossed lanes, and then smashed through the side barrier.

It got halfway through before it snagged and caught on twisted metal. The front wheels dangled above the river, and the whole car rocked back and forth.

Kevin screeched to a stop right behind it. He got out and sprinted forward. Other cars stopped as well, other drivers getting out to gawk or help, but Kevin didn't have time for them. Carefully, he climbed up on the twisted railing. Strong winds buffeted him from each side, and the metal was slick beneath his boots. He grabbed for a handhold on a support and leaned forward.

The police officer was unmoving behind the steering wheel, a trickle of blood coming out of her nose. She might already be dead.

"Get down!" one of the bystanders yelled. "Wait for the fire department!"

The patrol car slid forward a few inches, dangling even more treacherously over the rushing river.

Kevin leaned forward and rapped on the driver's window. "Wake up! Can you hear me?"

The police officer didn't move. Kevin pulled out his FRED. The King was still in the engine block, registering so high off the meter he was afraid the screen might crack. Ruins didn't like water; any minute now, it was going to jump. But if he fried the car with the driver still in it, he risked killing her.

The officer woke up, saw the danger she was in, and began shouting for help.

"Open the door!" Kevin ordered. "You can do it!"

But the door wouldn't open. The bridge railing kept it pinned shut.

"The window!" Kevin yelled.

The officer—her nametag said "McCoy"—tried the electric windows. They slid down only a few inches before stopping.

"Go get the fire department," she told Kevin, her voice cracking. "Don't get yourself killed."

"They're on their way," Kevin promised her. "I can hear them."

He could indeed hear them, far away but growing closer. Evening had come on quickly, leaving the shores dark and the river a noisy blackness. As if in response to the sirens, the patrol car began rocking precariously over the edge.

"Get back!" McCoy yelled.

"Do you have a hammer?" Kevin asked. Not just any hammer, but the special kind that could be used to smash car windows.

"I think—" McCoy reached toward the glove compartment, but the car rocked forward even more, and she gave a short scream.

"Okay, don't move," Kevin said. He turned his head, scanning the crowd. With great relief, he saw Ford arrive on his Harley, followed by a tow truck from Richie Venezuela's junkyard.

Ford dismounted. "Kevin, get down from there!"

"I'm not leaving!" Kevin yelled. To McCoy he said, "I'm not leaving you. Promise."

"You're a brave kid," McCoy said. "But I don't want you to get killed."

"I won't," Kevin said.

Richie, Gear, and Ford were running a tow chain toward the patrol car. The King might have sensed them coming—who knew what a King could see or hear?—and began rocking back and forth even more. The men were stymied in their attempt to get the chain around the bumper.

"I'm going to have to zap it," Ford said. "Grab tight!"

Kevin said to McCoy, "Hold on!" and threw his arms around the support beam.

But the King was already fleeing. It jumped out of the patrol car with an explosion of gold and purple fireworks that blasted across the bridge, past cars and bystanders and the fire truck arriving on scene. The force of it threw the car back a few feet, nearly flattening Gear, Richie, and Ford, but saving Officer McCoy.

The support under Kevin's feet groaned and gave way.

"Dad!" he yelled, and then he was falling toward the treacherous black water below.

CHAPTER TWENTY-THREE

I want to do more," Danny said as Mrs. Morris stopped for a four-way traffic stop. Outside, the sun was going down and the sky growing dark. Halloween pumpkins glowed outside a house that was also decorated with fake gravestones and skeletons. "I want to help you catch these things."

"We have plenty of people working on this," she promised him. "It's very dangerous, and I'd hate to see anything happen to you."

"But these things killed my friends!" he said.

She gave him a skeptical look. Okay, so maybe Ryan and Jackie hadn't been his friends. Danny struggled to find more words. "It's just...well, knowing these things are out there explains a lot. Like why so many people get killed in car accidents."

Mrs. Morris was sympathetic but firm. "People die in car accidents for many reasons, Danny. Teenage drivers often lack experience and judgment. Adult drivers multitask with their cell phones or are otherwise distracted. Elderly drivers continue to drive even when they have vision problems or can't respond quickly. These things we chase are dangerous, yes, but statistically speaking, humans are just as dangerous by themselves."

Danny didn't answer.

She accelerated and didn't speak again until they reached Roger's house.

"I guess I won't see you at school on Monday," he said, reaching for the door handle.

"Probably not," she said. "Though you can expect a visit from our home office. Some very stern men will come talk to you about the forms you signed. Remember, you're not allowed to discuss this with anyone. If word got out, people might start to panic."

"I won't tell anyone," he promised her. "Before you go, could you check my mom's car? I don't want to think one of those things is in it."

Mrs. Morris obliged. She used her phone to scan both his mother's Volvo and Roger's Lexus. Both registered less than 10.

"Try to forget," Mrs. Morris urged him. "Or at least not worry too much. When you graduate school, if you're still interested, you can come to work with us. It's a lot of travel, and a lot of hardship, but well worth the price. Good-bye, Danny."

She drove off to fight evil without him. She and the other guys and Kevin, too, which didn't seem fair—that Kevin was Danny's age but already living a life full of amazing, dangerous secrets.

He wondered if he would ever see Kevin again.

Danny trudged inside. Downstairs, the house was all cold and dark. Only Comet came to meet him, and that was with happy barks and tail wagging. Upstairs, his mother was putting on her makeup and jewelry for a fancy party.

"There you are," she said. "How was your day?"

He shrugged. "It was okay. Where are you going?"

"There's a party downtown for Country Harvest VIPs," she said. "Roger's helping set it up right now. Moon Senior and all the other singers will be there. Are you hungry? I put out money for pizza."

"Not so much," he said. His wrist was hurting, too, but he didn't mention that. "I'm going to go lie down for a while."

She came to him and felt his forehead. "Do you feel okay?"

Danny nodded.

"Just relax and watch some movies," she said. "Rachel's going to some party at Junior's, so you'll have the whole house to yourself. Tomorrow, for your birthday, we'll go out and have a big breakfast, okay?"

"Sure," Danny said.

He turned to leave her, but paused at the door. "Can I ask you something?"

She gave him a quizzical look. "Sure. What is it?"

Danny didn't know how to ask it. *Do you think I'm gay?* seemed entirely too blunt. That wasn't something you could just ask your mom. *Do other people think I'm gay?* was maybe a little more diplomatic. He tried more variations in his head: *Do I look like I want to kiss other boys? Do you think your only son is a faggot?*

Instead, he changed the topic completely.

"You always told me Dad's accident wasn't his fault," he said. "So it was definitely the other guy?"

Mom picked up a silver necklace and carefully put it around her neck. Her eyes were sad. "Does it matter?"

"Maybe."

She took her time answering. "The other man said his brakes failed, but the police mechanics said they were fine. Why are you thinking about that?"

He shrugged. "No reason."

"Danny." Mom stood and took both his hands. "I know it hasn't been easy. First we were a family of four, and then there were just the two of us, and now there's Roger and Rachel. But I really want this to work, and I want you to be happy."

Danny kissed her forehead. "I am," he lied. "I promise."

She left for the party twenty minutes later, leaving Danny alone in the big house. He put some ice on his wrist, which was still hurting, and scribbled down some lyrics for a new song. This time he wrote about Ruins, and people dying, and cars smashing into each other.

And Kevin. Kevin with his shaggy blond hair and leather jacket and how he'd saved Danny's life by zapping Roger's truck.

Danny's phone rang with calls from Laura, but he didn't answer them.

Instead, he ordered the pizza and ate three slices while looking at the computer archives of the *San Francisco Chronicle*. His dad's accident was just a small note buried in the middle of the paper. James Kelly and Michael Kelly, both killed. He tried looking up information on Ruins but found nothing. Secret government files, he figured. National security.

The phone rang again. This time it was Eric. He said, "Emily figured out more about your toy. She knows who made it."

Danny sat up against his desk so fast that he nearly knocked over the rest of the pizza. "She does?"

"Piedmont's a rich town, but there aren't that many people here interested in radio-controlled cars. She talked to the owner of Nicholas Toys downtown. He likes her because she spends so much money there. He gave her a name."

Danny grabbed a pencil. "Give it to me."

"Nope. I'll come pick you up. Be ready in ten minutes."

Sure enough, ten minutes later, Eric's Camaro was pulling into the driveway with music blaring from the stereo.

"You don't have to get involved in this," Danny said. "It could be dangerous, and I'm not kidding."

Eric shrugged. "Yeah, whatever. Dangerous toys. Get in."

"Can I drive?" Danny asked.

"No."

Danny climbed into the passenger seat. It was dark out now and colder than he thought. He should have worn a heavier jacket. "How far are we going?"

"Other side of town." Eric handed over a piece of paper and put the car in reverse. "What's so special about this toy, anyway? You looking for a new hobby?"

"Not exactly," Danny said. "I just think it's kind of cool."

"Now you sound like my sister."

Twenty minutes later, they stopped in front of an old Victorian house at the top of a spooky hill. The house's windows were dark and dusty. No lights were on. Overgrown bushes and trees shivered in the breeze, and Danny thought he saw bats flying in and out of the belfry.

"Now there's a house all done up for Halloween," Eric said.

Danny replied, "I think that's how it normally looks."

The driveway was gated, so Eric parked in the street, and they made their way up the overgrown walkway. The porch creaked loudly when Eric stepped on it. Yellowed newspapers lay piled by the door, and spider webs hung over the front door.

"Who'd you say this guy was?" Danny asked.

"Some retired guy from Detroit—" Eric yelped. "Look at that spider!"

The black spider hanging upside down above their heads was the biggest, ugliest one that Danny had ever seen—as big as a dinner plate, with bright red eyes. Electric eyes.

"That's no normal spider," Danny said.

The front door swung open on its own. Behind it were darkness and the smell of mold.

Eric asked, "Are we going in there?"

"You bet," Danny said and stepped inside.

CHAPTER TWENTY-FOUR

Eric said, "Wish we had a flashlight."

Danny fumbled around on the wall until he found three switches. The first one did nothing, nor did the second, but the third made the chandelier over them burst into light.

The minute the chandelier lit up, a toy police truck beeped on the stairway. A fire truck raced their way and stopped with its lights flashing. A black helicopter lifted off the scuffed hardwood floors and landed again. The noise of it made Eric step sideways against Danny, who nearly tripped over a small monster truck.

"Whoa!" Eric said. "What is this, some freaky toy store?"

Carefully, Danny picked up the monster truck. "I don't think they're regular toys."

A man's voice spoke from the far end of the hall. "Of course they're not!"

The owner of the voice stepped forward. He was an elderly man with long gray hair and hoop earrings in both ears. He wore a Muddy Waters T-shirt under his cardigan sweater and was carrying a circuit board in one hand.

"Are you Mr. Beaudreau?" Eric asked.

"Yes, that's me." The man stifled a deep, rattling cough. When he was done he said, "Do you know 2KEWLE? Have you seen him?"

The hope was so naked in his voice that Danny hated to disappoint him. "Not lately. But we'd like to talk to you about him."

Beaudreau coughed into a handkerchief. "You'd better come on back to the kitchen."

The "kitchen" was the largest and brightest room in the house. Somewhere there was a refrigerator and stove and sink, but almost every flat surface was covered with radio-controlled vehicles in various stages of assembly or disassembly. There were also dozens of cardboard boxes filled with spare tires, frames, wires, motors, boards, and other parts. The kitchen table itself was a workbench. A transistor radio in the middle of it was playing Janis Joplin.

"If you can find something to drink, you're welcome to it." Beaudreau coughed again, sounding like a man who'd smoked all his life and quit too late. He donned a pair of eyeglasses and squinted at them with a frown. "But be careful where you put it. They don't like water much. Scares them."

Eric took in all of the electronics and said, "My sister would love this place."

"Bring her, too." Beaudreau donned another pair of glasses. "Now, what's this about 2KEWLE? Has he been causing trouble?"

"You keep saying 'he,'" Danny said. "Like he's a person."

Beaudreau sat unsteadily on a stool. "Just like a person! All of them are."

Danny eyed the fire truck, police car, and other vehicles that had rolled to the doorway and were watching the humans.

"Like real people?" Eric asked. "Ghosts of real people?"

Danny remembered Ford's warnings about treason and federal law and kept his mouth shut.

Beaudreau picked up a circuit board and examined it carefully. Without looking at them, he asked, "Do you know your laws of thermodynamics? What happens when you have a high-energy system connected to one with lower energy? For instance, two adjacent rooms, one hot and one cold. You open the door and what happens?"

Danny rubbed the back of his head. "Energy migrates. The high energy—heat—moves to the low energy."

"And the cold air goes to the hot room," Eric said.

"No," Danny told him. "Not spontaneously."

Beaudreau lifted his head and beamed at Danny. "Someone's been paying attention in school."

"Is that what you're talking about?" Danny asked. "Things that come from a world of higher energy into ours?"

Beaudreau straightened his back. He put the circuit board down. "I'll tell you a story. About a factory. The industry of America, where Henry Ford's dreams came true. One day, the workers punched a hole in the wall between two rooms, and no one's ever found a way to close it. They had to shut down the factory and open up another, thousands of miles away. But even then, another hole opened. Do you understand?"

"Do you mean car factories?" Danny said. "Like Detroit?"

"All my life, I worked in Flint," Beaudreau said. "Gave it everything I had. Then General Motors closed the plants and the whole town collapsed. But that didn't shut the breaches. Mexico, China, Russia—wherever there's an assembly line, they punch through."

"My dad was born in Detroit," Danny said. "His father and grandfather worked in the factories."

"That explains it!" Beaudreau said. "You play guitar, too?"

"A little," Danny said. "Explains what?"

Beaudreau coughed into his handkerchief. Danny couldn't be sure, but he thought he saw flecks of blood in it.

"Maybe you should see a doctor," Danny said.

Beaudreau waved the handkerchief. "No doctor can help me now."

Eric said, "I don't understand. What are you two talking about?"

"Breaches and holes," Beaudreau said. "You carry Detroit in your blood, young man. The blues and the assembly lines. No wonder 2KEWLE likes you."

Danny asked, "Is 2KEWLE one of the bad guys?"

Beaudreau looked offended. "Of course not! Who have you been listening to? Those fools who work for the government?" He broke off into another cough, and Danny was alarmed at the rattling sound he made when he breathed. Beaudreau continued, "The Department of Transportation has one mission only: destruction. I tried to tell them. Bureaucrats. They never listen."

Outside the house, metal clattered.

"That'll be him now," Beaudreau said.

The cat flap in the kitchen door opened. 2KEWLE bumped over the sill, rolled weakly toward Beaudreau, and died.

Chapter Twenty-five

It's all right," Beaudreau said around some more coughing. "He just needs a new battery. He's supposed to come home before it's too late, but sometimes he pushes himself too far."

He scooped up 2KEWLE, put him on the table, and flipped him over. A few deft moves and one battery later, 2KEWLE revved back to life. He popped a little wheelie and beeped his horn.

Eric asked, "Are you trying to say there's some kind of alien from another world hanging out in that toy?"

"He's not a toy," Beaudreau said.

"Can he find the other ones?" Danny asked. "The ones the government is looking for?"

2KEWLE beeped his horn three times.

Beaudreau sat back on his stool and crossed his arm. "Kings, eh? Who have you been talking to, boy?"

Eric said, "Yeah, who?"

Danny shrugged. "Some people."

"Some people." Beaudreau coughed again, deep and hacking. "Federal agents, it sounds like. Don't believe everything they tell you. They've got their own plans, their own secrets. They see only black and white, and no shades of gray. If they had their way, they'd destroy all of these Ruins too."

The tiny machines in the doorway all rolled backward.

"Two of our classmates were killed last night," Danny said. "More people could die."

Eric said, "Now you're sounding melodramatic."

"Kings always kill again." Beaudreau's eyebrows drew together in consternation. "But such a dangerous job is not for boys. You should leave it to the professionals."

"Bureaucrats," Danny reminded him.

After a moment's indecision, Beaudreau nodded. He looked down at 2KEWLE. "What do you think? Can you help them?"

2KEWLE popped another wheelie.

"That means yes," Beaudreau said.

❖

Eric said, "I can't believe I've got some alien-possessed toy leading me around town."

"Think of it as a special kind of GPS system," Danny suggested.

They had 2KEWLE propped on the dashboard. It was almost nine o'clock at night, and there wasn't much traffic on the road.

"How are we supposed to stop this King thing?" Eric asked.

"I don't know. And you're not supposed to know, okay? This is all secret government stuff."

Eric squinted at him. "Did you get some crazy part-time job that I don't know about?"

Danny tried not to squirm. "It doesn't matter. Just remember, if you start blabbing, I end up in jail for treason. Let's just find this thing, okay?"

2KEWLE beeped agreement.

They turned left and right, winding through the streets of Piedmont, until 2KEWLE started rocking back and forth in excitement. Eric led them further up into the hills on the east side of town, into richer and richer neighborhoods, until they came to a mansion that looked like a mini White House plucked down on a Tennessee hilltop. Dozens and dozens of cars were parked in the driveway and on the lawn. Country music blasted out of the windows.

Eric snorted. "Good job. This thing brought us right to Junior Conway's party."

Danny groaned. "You're kidding."

Eric parked on the edge of a dirt road that swung around to a barn and pastures. Danny doubted that any Conway ever actually milked a cow, but appearances were important. The minute Danny opened his door, 2KEWLE jumped down and roared through the grass.

Hey!" Danny shouted. "Where are you going?"

2KEWLE beeped its horn and disappeared under the wheels of an SUV.

"Stupid thing," Danny said. "Help me look for him."

They searched for several minutes, looking under trucks and cars, but 2KEWLE was nowhere to be found. Finally, Eric said, "Look, it's a party. Maybe he went inside for a beer."

"Don't be silly."

"Well, I need a drink," Eric said. "All this crazy talk has made me thirsty. You coming?"

"No. I'll meet you later."

Left alone, Danny kept looking for 2KEWLE. "Come on, come out. What are you doing?"

But the toy didn't show itself.

CHAPTER TWENTY-SIX

Just as Kevin was about to plummet into the raging water and rocks below the bridge, a hand grabbed his arm and yanked him forward. He fell toward the deck of the bridge and landed in his father's strong, rough arms.

His father, who seemed determined to squeeze him to death.

"Next time you do something this dumb," Ford said into Kevin's right ear, "I'm going to kill you myself."

Other voices; other helping hands; gradually Kevin found himself sitting in the cab of the tow truck. He wasn't wet, but someone put a blanket around him anyway. The police were busy holding back traffic while the firemen and paramedics treated Officer McCoy. The King was gone, which was bad news.

Plus, everyone had seen the purple and gold explosion as it catapulted into the air, which was even worse news when it came to national security secrets.

"Are we all going to get fired?" he asked as his dad handed him a cup of coffee from a thermos.

"Don't you worry about that," Ford said.

Kevin drank the coffee gratefully. He was ridiculously cold, even with the blanket around him. "But everyone saw it."

"People don't know what they see," Ford replied. He squeezed the bridge of his nose, looking exhausted. "Kevin, I know you blame yourself for Dallas, but you can't take risks like this. I can't lose you."

All of a sudden, the dark swirls in Kevin's cup looked pretty fascinating. "This wasn't about Dallas."

Ford squeezed his shoulder. "Dallas was a mistake. I don't hold you responsible. I hold myself responsible because I'm the leader of this team."

"But I screwed up!" Kevin insisted. "I should have been faster, driven better—"

Ford shook his head. "I say that every day about the accident that killed your mother. But we're not stronger than the Kings. We're not faster. We do the best we can, and we move on. But I won't be able to move on if you get yourself killed."

Kevin blinked against sudden wetness in his eyes. "That kind of works both ways, Dad."

Ford gave him another hug.

Gear came over, interrupting the moment. "The cops need you, Ford. Flash them your badge, will you?"

Ford squeezed Kevin's shoulder again before leaving.

Eventually, Officer McCoy was taken away in an ambulance, the damaged patrol car was towed away, the inspectors cleared the bridge for reopening, and traffic began to clear away. No one was paying attention to Kevin when his phone rang. Danny's number. He slid out of Richie Venezuela's truck and walked a few feet away.

"Hi," Danny said. "You busy?"

"Not so much," Kevin said carefully. "Why?"

"There's a party. You should come."

No one had ever asked Kevin to come to a party. It was such a new experience that he wasn't sure he'd heard Danny correctly. "A what?"

"A party. Up at Moon Conway's house."

"I don't know who that is."

"You should come," Danny insisted.

Kevin wanted to yell a little bit. Didn't Danny understand how important finding the King was? Kevin had a job to do. He wasn't in town to go to parties or get drunk or do whatever suburban kids did when their parents weren't looking over their shoulders. This wasn't about recreation or pleasure.

"I think I might have found 2KEWLE," Danny added.

That changed everything.

❖

"I'm not going to turn you in," Danny said into the darkness, hoping 2KEWLE was listening. "I just need to ask some questions."

The toy didn't answer.

While waiting for Kevin to show up, Danny hiked around to the pool. Girls in skinny jeans and boys in cowboy hats were dancing and drinking. Open doors led into the ballroom. Danny couldn't believe Moon even had a ballroom. Everything inside was dark and hot and pulsing with light, and the crowd was so dense that Danny had trouble making out the details of faces.

But he knew who these kids were, even without seeing their faces. They were the cool kids from Piedmont—the jocks, the cheerleaders, kids whose parents had money or fame. Not him. He didn't care. When he was an adult, he planned to be famous for his music, not because of who he knew or what parties he got invited to.

He got about a dozen steps inside before he ran into Junior.

"You." Junior's eyes were not quite focused, and his drawl was heavier than usual. Too much to drink already. "What are you doing here?"

"Just crashing through," Danny said.

Eric joined them with two plastic cups in hand. "We hear you were auctioning off your car, Junior. Raffle tickets to benefit the football team's brain damage fund."

Junior's expression slid into disbelief. "My car? Who's auctioning my car?"

"Some girl outside," Eric said.

Junior lurched off. Eric said, "Here you go," and handed Danny a cup. He sniffed it, smelled some kind of alcohol, and put it on the nearest table.

"His parents let him have parties like this?" Danny asked, climbing the wide circular stairway.

Eric shrugged. "Moon Senior's at Country Harvest all weekend. Besides, they've got houses like I've got zits. Probably don't use this one half the time."

A pretty girl in a low top came down the stairs toward Danny. "Aren't you Junior's cousin?"

"No," he said.

She sashayed off down the stairs, disappointed.

"Idiot." Eric punched Danny's arm. "When someone asks if you're the rich, famous kid's cousin, you say yes!"

Eric followed the girl. Danny bit back impatience. What was taking Kevin so long? He should go back to waiting outside. He turned on the stairs and found his way blocked by Laura, who was wearing a low-cut red shirt and a big grin.

"You came!" She grabbed his hands. "All day I was calling you!"

Danny recoiled at the smell of beer on her breath. "You've been drinking."

Laura threw her arms around his neck. "Yes! A lot!"

"Come on. Let's go upstairs where it's quiet." Danny led her to the second-floor landing, where she leaned against a wall and nearly knocked over a side table.

"Easy," Danny said, rescuing the table. "How much did you drink?"

"Not enough." Laura pulled Danny closer and played with the buttons on his shirt. "It's okay. I feel great. It's better this way."

Passing strangers jostled Danny and made him step closer.

"Why's it better, Laura?"

"You know, always having to be good." She sighed. "Don't you get tired of it? Do this, do that, babysit, get good grades, all the time. I'm so tired of that. Come on this way. I want to show you something."

She pulled him into a guest bedroom and closed the door.

CHAPTER TWENTY-SEVEN

Danny had not, in his wildest dreams, imagined his day would end like this: a nicely furnished bedroom, country music pounding through the walls, Laura backing him against the wall and kissing his mouth like she wanted to eat him alive.

He wanted to like the kissing. Or the way, her firm breasts pressed against him. He put his hands on her silky hair and smooth back and waited for something special to flow through him, like electricity. Surely, bisexual was better than gay, right?

Nothing happened except that Laura made little happy noises and Danny's body remained uninterested, maybe even repulsed.

She broke off with a grin and drew him backward toward the bed. "I've been waiting for this," she said. Light from outside the house illuminated her as she pulled her blouse off and revealed a lacy pink bra. "You and me, and haven't we waited long enough?"

Danny swallowed hard, his throat tight. "We haven't done barely anything."

"I know!" Laura grabbed his hands again and darted in for a kiss. Her tongue touched his. "But I've got a condom and I'm ready."

He almost laughed. Not at the sincerity in her voice (even if she was a little drunk), or the way she was stripping off her jeans now. None of that was funny. But he'd convinced himself, since moving to Piedmont, that he could fake it. That he could spend his high school years dating girls and no one would know the difference, not even himself. That was practically hysterical.

Still, he had to find a way to turn her down without letting her know the real reason why.

"You know I want to," he said, but his voice cracked in the middle of it. Stupid conscience. "Laura, now's not the best time."

"Sure it is." She kicked her jeans away and stretched out on the bed, one hand lifted toward him. "Come on."

He sat. She curved upward, kissed him again. Danny wished that his phone would ring, or someone would barge in, or maybe an asteroid would plummet through the ceiling.

No such luck.

"I can't," he said as her fingernails curled around the button of his jeans. "Not tonight."

"Boys can do it anytime," she insisted.

A brilliant solution popped into his head. "I've got that thing. You know, jock itch."

Laura's fingers stopped moving. She gave him a disbelieving look. "You've got what?"

"It's all red and sore," he said, trying to sound embarrassed. "I've got this cream, but it's contagious until the doctor says so."

She giggled. "You do not. I don't believe it. Let me see."

"You'll get it under your fingernails," Danny insisted. He made himself kiss her on the lips and then said, "Or get it somewhere else, and you'll have to tell the doctor how."

Her head was tilted back now. He could see she didn't want to believe it. He felt bad she'd built up this special night, if only in her own head, and here he was, ruining it. But then she sank back on the pillows and giggled again.

"Jock itch," she said. "Poor baby."

Danny helped her get her clothes back on, and let her cling to his side, and maybe there were some more kisses he could tolerate, and then he tugged her out into the hallway. Some kids out there gave him a knowing smirk. Everyone knew, or thought they knew, what had been going on. It occurred to him that this could work to his advantage for a little while, but sooner or later, his fictitious rash was going to clear up and then what? He couldn't fake medical incapacity forever.

"Let's get more drunk," Laura proposed.

Before he could disagree, a girl's angry voice cut through the noise and din around them.

"I said no!"

Danny turned to see Rachel storming out of another bedroom, her blouse half-pulled off her shoulders. Her hair was disheveled and she looked furious.

"But, honey!" The boy following her wasn't Junior, but instead a Piedmont Prep football player named Buddy Hunt. Danny didn't like Buddy, but lots of people did. He was number two on the team, but would have been number one if it weren't for Moon Conway's fame.

Rachel spun around in her high heels. She wagged her finger at Buddy. "Don't even say it! Don't even think it!"

Buddy spread his arms wide, no doubt aware of all the spectators around them. "But you wanted it!"

"I don't want anything from you," Rachel said, and stormed off toward the stairs.

Danny tried to follow her, but the crowd was too thick and Laura was tugging him in another direction. The party had grown larger in the short time Danny had been upstairs. Some of the new kids had a hard look about them, as if they were just out for themselves and whatever free booze they could score. They were the kind of guests who stole stuff or jammed up the toilets just for the fun of it, and would maybe throw a sofa into the pool, or damage the property in other ways.

Surely, Junior was accustomed to throwing the kind of parties where opportunists came knocking.

Or maybe he wasn't. Maybe Junior didn't know how to tell the difference between friends and hangers-on, the kind who would take advantage of a rich star's son.

"I'm getting more beer," Laura said, and slid away in the confusion.

Danny's phone rang.

"I'm outside," Kevin said. "Where's the toy?"

"Meet me by the garage," Danny said.

The fresh air outside was a big relief, as was the solitude. The garage was a monstrous, six-bay building, locked tight but lit up inside to show off Moon Conway Senior's car collection. Kevin was standing at one corner, hands jammed in his pockets, looking like someone who'd rather be anywhere else in the world. Just seeing him was a relief. Here was someone who wasn't drunk, wasn't even drinking. Someone Danny didn't have to lie to, at least not when it came to jock itch. For a very brief moment, he wondered what it would be like to bring Kevin inside, to hold his hand while other people watched, to dance one slow dance in the middle of the room.

But that was like wishing for the impossible.

"You've got lipstick on your face," Kevin said.

Danny wiped at his cheek. "Someone tried to kiss me."

"And on your neck, too," Kevin said. "She must have been pretty interested in your heterosexuality."

Danny grimaced. "Can you shut up about that?"

Kevin shrugged. "You said you saw 2KEWLE?"

"By the cars in the lawn," he said, deliberately leading him away from the last place he'd seen the buggy.

❖

Kevin had told Ford and the rest of the team that Danny had questions about the Ruins, nothing more.

"Tell him you'll answer tomorrow," Ford said.

"No, it's okay," Kevin replied. He didn't want to tell them that Danny was calling about 2KEWLE; otherwise, they might all want to come along. "It won't take long."

"You sure you're up for it?" Ford asked.

Kevin rolled his eyes. "Dad, I didn't fall off a bridge, I *almost* fell off. Big difference."

So now here he was, at this big fancy mansion on the hill. He hadn't expected how many people would be here or the sheer awfulness of the country music blaring from inside. He almost wished he'd put on nicer jeans and a cleaner shirt, but it wasn't as if he was going inside. He didn't need to make a fashion statement out on the dark lawn, under hazy clouds and scattered stars, as he scanned cars and trucks with his FRED.

"You sure you saw it?" he asked Danny.

Danny was standing right behind him "Pretty sure."

The blue pickup in front of Kevin registered 15. The white SUV beside it was a 23.

"Can I ask you something about the Ruins?" Danny asked, still very close behind him.

"What about them?"

"Like where they come from. What they want. I mean, has anyone ever asked them?"

Kevin almost dropped the FRED. "Ask them? Like you ask a rabid dog before it bites you?"

"But maybe they're not rabid," Danny said. "Maybe they're just misunderstood."

The next truck registered 35. Kevin paused to rescan it. "That's ridiculous. They're like fleas. Mindless. Just jumping around and carrying diseases. Trust me, I've been doing this for years."

Up at the house, the music changed tempo, to something slow and romantic.

Danny wasn't giving up on his idea, though. "Maybe the thing that's in 2KEWLE is different from the others. Maybe it's not a flea or a rabid dog but just got stuck here and is trying to help."

"Ruins don't help," Kevin snapped. "Ever. They kill."

He turned around. Danny was so close behind him that they collided, and Kevin had to grab his arms before Danny went stumbling backward. But he dropped his grip quickly, because he remembered the whole not-officially-gay thing.

"Sorry," Danny said, but Kevin didn't know if it was for standing so close or for his silly ideas.

"Did you really see that buggy or did you just want to ask me stupid questions?" Kevin asked.

Danny's chin lifted. "They're not stupid. The questions or the Ruins. Since when does the government tell the whole truth about anything?"

Kevin shook his head. "Now you sound like some conspiracy nut."

"It is a conspiracy! The government knows something that can get people killed every day," Danny said. "How do you know that there's not more to the story?"

Kevin pocketed his FRED. He really didn't have time for this, and he'd been foolish to come. "I'm going back. There's no King here."

He stalked off a few feet before Danny said, "Wait! I need to tell you something."

Kevin wasn't particularly interested, but something in Danny's voice caught him and made him turn around. "What now?"

"It's just—" Danny faltered. He looked miserable, but also determined not to back down. "You were right. About the thing that I'm not. Officially."

Kevin waited for more.

"I realize that it's stupid to pretend otherwise," Danny said tightly. "I don't think I can tell anyone, though. Not in this town. It's not like San Francisco was."

Kevin gazed past Danny to the mansion and then back again. The wind was kicking up, the clouds growing thicker overhead. "So you lied to me."

Danny squared his shoulders. "I lied to myself first."

Kevin thought about that. "There's got to be other gay kids around this town. You're not alone."

"I don't know how to tell my mom," Danny said. "Or what my stepdad will say."

"I don't have a lot of advice," Kevin replied. His father had always been good with it. They'd never lived anywhere long enough for any neighbors to notice or care, or for classmates and teachers to give him hell.

Danny stepped closer. "I think I could have pretended a lot longer if you hadn't come to town."

Kevin felt a little thrill of pleasure at that. Carefully, he asked, "Are you saying it's my fault?"

Danny said, "Yes. Your hair's too long and that leather jacket is too...leathery."

This time, Kevin's smile slipped out. "I don't think that's a word."

"I made it up," Danny said. "Can I kiss you?"

"Yeah," Kevin said.

But before they could, a girl's voice spoke snidely from nearby. "Well, lookie here. I knew I was right."

Rachel.

Chapter Twenty-eight

D anny was mortified.

"What are you, spying on me?" he demanded, glaring at his stepsister. Of all the times to interrupt! And of all the things to interrupt, too. His first official guy kiss ever, and she'd ruined the whole thing.

"I don't care about your love life," she said, annoyed. "I need a ride home and someone saw you come this way."

Danny said, "Ask one of your friends!"

"They're all drunk," she said. Her gaze switched to Kevin. "You could drive me."

"No spare helmet," he said.

Rachel's eyes went right back to Danny. "Find Eric. Tell him you want to go now. I'm so sick of these people I want to throw up on them."

"Not my problem," Danny said defiantly. But a moment later, he realized it would entirely be his problem if Rachel blabbed her big mouth.

Kevin patted Danny's arm. "Go on, take her. I've got to get back to my dad before he starts worrying I've fallen off a bridge again."

"Again?" Danny asked.

"Long story," Kevin said. "Call me later."

He slipped away through the cars. Rachel said, "Finally," and turned to march back toward the mansion. Danny followed her reluctantly, irritated and worried at the same time.

"Are you going to tell people?" he asked.

"That I caught my stepbrother trying to kiss a guy?" Rachel asked flippantly. "Who cares?"

"I care!"

"Your secret is safe with me, Romeo," she said.

He didn't know if he could trust her and was halfway sure he couldn't. Danny almost pressured her for more of a promise, but as they reached the house, a girl's shout cut off any chance of conversation.

"They're going to race!" the girl cried out. "Junior's going to race!"

A tide of onlookers carried Danny and Rachel to the big circular driveway. Junior was behind the wheel of his yellow Porsche, revving the engines. Buddy Hunt was gunning a cherry red Corvette.

"What are you doing, Junior?" someone shouted.

"Defending the family honor!" Junior yelled back.

Rachel stalked out to the middle ground between the two cars, her hands on her hips. "Moon Junior, you get your butt out of that car. You're drunk."

"We ain't racing far, honey! Just down to the old barn and back."

Danny could see the barn at the far end of the Conway's property, at the very end of a slope. The dirt lane looked barely wide enough for one car, never mind two. He could already imagine one or both of them sliding off the embankment and flipping in the grass, maybe catching fire and exploding.

Laura and Eric had come out of the house and were standing in the crowd behind Danny. Laura said, "They've got to be crazy."

Junior said to Rachel, "Drop the flag, darling!"

Rachel had to be aware of everyone watching and judging her. He was relieved when she shook her head and snagged the keys from the Porsche's ignition.

"You're an idiot." She flung the keys away, far into the bushes.

The crowd booed, but she didn't appear to care. Instead, she stalked over to Danny and said, "Let's go."

Danny turned to Eric. "Can you drive?"

Eric fumbled for his keys. "No problem! But I'm a little drunk."

"You drive," Rachel said. "I won't tell. It's only a few miles."

Eric burped. "Good idea! I won't tell, either."

"I want to leave, too," Laura announced. "All the fun part's over."

Danny hesitated. Rachel was right. It was only about three or four miles to home. If he drove with perfect attention to traffic lights, didn't break the speed limit, and had the best luck ever, he could drop Laura off, return Eric and his car to Eric's house, and walk home with Rachel before his mom and Roger got back from their party.

"Get in," Danny said.

Eric claimed shotgun. The girls got into the backseat. Danny slid behind Eric's steering wheel and relished the feel of it under his fingers. For three years, he'd missed this.

"It works better if you turn it on," Eric said.

Danny turned the ignition. Slowly, he eased the Camaro off the grass and down the road. Moon Senior's estate receded into trees and moonlight.

"You drive like my grandma." Eric burped. "What happened to Captain Carjack?"

"Who's Captain Carjack?" Laura asked from the backseat.

"Him."

"Shut up," Danny said. There was a stop sign at the end of the street. He wanted to run it, but instead he slowed down. "He's delusional."

"Captain Carjack of California!" This time Eric's burp was accompanied by a ruder noise.

Rachel was already on her cell phone, messaging her friends. "Will you drive faster? He's going to stink up everything!"

Eric made another noise. "Beer makes my stomach upset."

Laura was hanging on to the back of Danny's seat. "You carjacked someone in California?"

"No," Danny said. He crossed the intersection and started down the hill. No other cars were out, for which he was grateful. He could feel his foot drawn to the gas pedal and had to move it aside before his worst impulses took over. "Don't listen to him. He's delusional."

Eric leaned forward between the front seats. "No, honestly. Honesty is important, right? Be honest with her. You can't drive because you're a felon."

"Tell the truth, Danny," Rachel said. "She's going to find out sooner or later."

Danny gritted his teeth. "I'm not a felon."

Which was sort of true. To be precise, he was a juvenile offender. But if wanting to open the passenger door and abandon Eric and Rachel in the middle of nowhere was a crime, he was already convicted.

"Danny," Laura said, drawing out the syllables in a most annoying way. "Did you tell them about your jock itch?"

Before he could answer, a twin pair of headlights appeared in the rearview mirror. Junior's yellow Porsche raced up behind them and pulled alongside Danny, smack dab in the incoming traffic lane.

"Oh, crap," he said, because that was just what the night needed—Junior chasing Rachel down or looking for a fight.

Eric belched. "Looks like he found his keys."

Junior rolled down his window and yelled. "Hey, Rachel! Come on! Don't go away mad!"

Rachel refused to look over at him. She said, "Just ignore him. He'll go away."

"I think he wants to race," Eric said. "Floor it!"

"No." Danny rolled down his window. "Junior, go home!"

"I want Rachel!" Junior yelled.

Danny kept going down Turkey Hill. The road was straight and long. Junior's Porsche kept pace as he beeped and yelled. Danny went faster.

"You're going to kill us," Laura said, bracing herself.

"Don't kill my car," Eric said.

Danny protested, "I'm not the one doing anything!"

Rachel's phone rang. She said into it, "Junior, stop it! I'm not going to talk to you!"

Junior was nudging into Danny's lane, trying to get him to pull into the extremely narrow shoulder. Danny felt himself being squeezed over. Gravel spun under the right tires, but he didn't lose control, didn't cede it. Headlights appeared ahead of them as some unsuspecting motorist headed up Turkey Hill.

"You're going to get us killed!" Rachel shouted into her phone.

Danny wasn't sure that Junior saw the oncoming driver. If they collided, one or both of them might spin into him. They might crash over the guardrail into the ravines and houses below, or blow up in some fiery explosion.

In just a few seconds, they might all die.

"Hold on," he warned them. "This is going to be tight."

He braked, groped for a gear stick that wasn't there, and fell far back so Junior could move into his lane.

The oncoming car blasted its horn now, a long, steady blare of noise that sounded like panic. Junior braked, swerved into the lane ahead of Danny, and missed the stranger by what looked like only inches. Then Junior braked again, the idiot. Danny had no choice but to either brake, swerve, or ram into him.

He tried braking and swerving both, but the Camaro fishtailed, bounced off rock, slid into the guardrail, and plunged downward.

Danny heard Laura and Rachel screaming. He probably screamed, too. The Camaro sailed downward, touched ground, bounced, rattled, sailed again. Tree branches scraped against the roof and punched through the windows. The front end of the car barreled into dark, cold water that flooded up through the floorboards.

"Out, out!" Danny yelled.

"We're going to drown!" Eric tried shouldering open his door, but it was jammed. "We're sinking!"

CHAPTER TWENTY-NINE

In the dark, wet, cold of the wreck Rachel said, "We're not sinking, idiot."

She sounded a lot calmer than Danny felt. Danny peered over the steering wheel and saw she was right. The pond they'd landed in was too shallow to swallow the car. That knowledge didn't stop his heart from thudding wildly inside his chest. He couldn't believe they weren't dead.

Maybe they really had died. Maybe they were ghosts.

"I think I'm bleeding," Eric said, making a strange snuffling noise.

Danny flipped on the dome light. Eric's nose was bleeding. Rachel and Laura both were unhurt. Danny's wrist hurt, but no worse than it had all day. He reached over, fished some napkins out of the glove compartment, and gave them to Eric.

"Let's get out," Rachel said. "I'm getting wet."

The doors were jammed with mud, but the electric windows still worked. They climbed out and slipped down into the water and mud. The night was cold and windy all around them. They'd landed in a deep ravine thick with trees and bushes, with the Camaro half in and half out of the pond and no clear path up to the road or down the hillside.

"I've got to call my mom," Laura said shakily, flipping open her cell phone.

But she couldn't get a signal. None of them could.

Danny said, "I'll climb out. Go for help."

"Me, too," Rachel said.

He looked at her shoes. "You can't climb in those."

She slipped them off. "Lead on."

The first dozen feet up the slope weren't so bad, though he couldn't grab for branches well with his left hand and needed the right hand for the flashlight he'd found in the glove compartment. Rachel was far more nimble, though the mud under their feet was slippery and torn up from the Camaro's descent. It was several long minutes before they reached the road, where Rachel used her phone to call 911.

A fire engine showed up four minutes later, followed by a police car.

"Our friends are down there," Rachel said, pointing down the ravine. "My brother here swerved to avoid a deer."

The firefighters and policemen immediately set to work. Danny gaped at Rachel and demanded, "You're lying for Junior?"

She lifted her chin defiantly. "I'd do the same for you. Getting him in trouble isn't going to make things any better. Just say it was a deer."

"He forced us off the road!"

"It was an accident. If you get Junior arrested, there will be all kinds of problems, and that won't be good for his daddy's career or for mine."

"No." Danny folded his arms. "I'm not going to protect him."

"It's a little lie," Rachel said. "You've got your secret gay boyfriend, and this is just something in return. You owe me."

Danny's fists clenched at his side.

Soon, the firefighters had Eric and Laura back up on the road, though it was going to be up to a tow truck to retrieve the Camaro. Neither Eric nor Laura were hurt. Rachel pulled them both aside to tell them to lie about Junior. A burly policeman came over to give Danny a field sobriety test.

The cop explained the procedures and then said, "Extend your arms, extend your index fingers, and bring both of them to the tip of your nose."

Embarrassed and annoyed, Danny carefully brought his fingers to his nose. His left wrist twinged as he did so, but he ignored it.

"Say the alphabet backwards from Z," the cop said.

Just then, Roger Rat's black Mercedes pulled up behind the fire engine, and Danny's night went from bad to worse.

Chapter Thirty

Roger parked on the shoulder. When he got out, he looked tremendously angry. He saw Danny but went directly to Rachel, who threw her arms around him.

"Daddy!" she said. "I was so scared."

Mom got out and came to Danny. She looked cold in her evening gown and jacket, and the expression on her face was just as angry and worried as Roger's.

"Are you all right?" she asked.

"Yeah," he muttered.

"I'm his mother," she said to the cop. "Carol Kelly Anderson."

The cop said, "It doesn't look like he was drinking, ma'am. He says he swerved to avoid a deer and the other kids confirmed it."

Danny glanced over at Eric and Laura. Neither of them would meet his gaze.

"Trouble is," the cop continued, "he doesn't have a driver's license."

Roger came over with Rachel in tow. Her mascara had streaked down her face from tears, and she wouldn't meet Danny's eyes.

"Rachel's going home to her mother's," Roger said. "We can clear all this up later, when people have calmed down."

Mom's eyebrows drew together and creased into a worry line. "I'd like to clear up some of it now. Rachel, was Danny drinking tonight?"

Rachel was peering down at her damaged high heel shoes. "No, ma'am."

That, at least, was the truth.

Mom said, "Rachel, were you drinking?"

Roger said, "Not here, Carol."

"Yes, here," Mom said firmly. "Danny made a mistake tonight, and he's going to pay for it. But he's not the only one who made bad decisions."

Rachel tugged on her sleeve. "Daddy, can't we go now? It's really cold."

Roger looked at the police officer and his nametag. "Is there anything more you need, Officer Johnson?"

"No, sir," the cop said. "Except your son here better see to his wrist. Looks like a sprain."

Danny looked down at his wrist in surprise. It was swollen and red, and now that he was paying attention, it really did hurt.

"It's okay," he assured his mother.

She frowned. "You probably need X-rays."

Which is how Danny and Mom ended up in the emergency room while Roger took Rachel to her mom. Mom handled all the paperwork at the admitting desk while Danny sat slumped in the bright, noisy waiting room. He was still mad about Junior and being blamed for something that wasn't his fault.

Mom came back from the desk and sat beside him.

"It shouldn't be long," she said, which was optimistic. The waiting room was full with sick people, and a crying baby, and a woman who looked very pregnant. Mom tapped her golden shoes on the linoleum and fixed her eyes on the TV bolted to a high shelf. "I want you to know that I'm glad you're okay. But you, Roger, and I are going to have to have a long series of talks about what happened tonight."

Danny sank lower into his seat.

It didn't help things at all that another police officer showed up to get more information just as Roger returned from dropping Rachel off. Mom, Roger, and the cop all conferred in the corner, sending Danny looks every now and then. He could imagine what they were saying about him, and none of it was good. It was a relief when a tall, gray-haired nurse named Barbara came to collect him.

"I'll be with you in a minute," Mom promised Danny.

Barbara took him through some swinging doors to a large area separated into cubicles by white curtains. She helped him sit on an exam table, and in quick succession took his pulse, stuck a thermometer in his ear, and measured his blood pressure.

"The doctor will be here soon," she said before leaving.

Soon was a relative term. Danny sat on the table for nearly a half hour, no sign of a physician. Maybe everyone had forgotten about him. He was debating getting up and walking out when his phone rang. Kevin's number flashed on the screen.

"Are you in the hospital?" Kevin demanded, sounding both worried and angry. "I just left you! What happened?"

"Nothing," Danny said. "A little ditch. A little accident. How did you know?"

"The police scanners. We monitor all of them. Was it the King?"

"No. It was Moon Junior being an idiot."

"But you're okay?"

"Yeah." Danny decided not to mention his wrist. "I'll be going home soon."

"Go home, stay put, and stay out of trouble," Kevin said. "Call me tomorrow."

"Okay," Danny said, thinking it was kind of nice that Kevin cared enough to sound mad at him.

Things got less nice when the doctor announced that Danny's wrist had a hairline fracture and they put it in a soft cast. He definitely wasn't going to be practicing guitar for a while. The drive home was a blur. Roger and Mom talked in low voices that he couldn't hear over the sound of Moon Conway crooning on the radio. When they got home, everyone trudged inside.

Comet met them, barking and spinning in circles.

"I'll take him out to pee," Mom said to Danny. "Go to bed and we'll talk about all this in the morning."

Roger said, "We've got to be out of the house by eight for the Country Harvest breakfast."

"Yes, I know," Mom said, sounding impatient.

Danny hauled himself upstairs. He was too tired and disappointed to do anything but toe off his shoes, throw himself on the bed and stare up at the ceiling. Eric's car was wrecked, Danny would probably have to go to court again, Junior was going to get off scot-free, 2KEWLE was nowhere around, and the King was still on the loose.

On the other hand, Kevin had almost kissed him. That was the best part of the day.

Comet came in and jumped up onto the bed with wet feet.

"Good boy," Danny said.

The dog licked Danny's face and settled against his arm. Danny reached over to turn off the light and saw the digital clock: 12:05 a.m.

"And happy birthday to me," he said.

CHAPTER THIRTY-ONE

2KEWLE was not having a good night.

He'd hitchhiked with Danny and Eric up to the mansion at Junior's, sensing the King's presence like an enormous blinking light on the horizon. At the party, he'd had to roll along dozens of cars until he found the one he was looking for: a cherry red Corvette with custom wheels.

King #5 roused inside the engine and peered at 2KEWLE with disdain. He'd found this car after leaping out of the police car on the bridge; he liked it and wanted to stay.

2KEWLE rolled forward and beeped for Danny.

"What are you?" asked a voice, and 2KEWLE found himself lifted in the air. "Ain't you cute? My little brother might like you."

2KEWLE beeped and struggled, but Buddy Hunt didn't care. He casually tossed him into his trunk and then turned around to yell at Junior.

"Hey, Junior! Want to race?"

The race didn't happen, but that didn't cheer 2KEWLE much. He was still stuck in the Corvette's trunk while Buddy drove home. He could feel the King lurking in the engine, enjoying the ride. He expected it to take over and maybe ram them into a tree or a concrete barrier. Kings liked to do that. But this King was quiet, maybe gathering up its strength, and Buddy reached home safely.

The Corvette was left in the driveway overnight.

2KEWLE threw himself at the trunk latch for hours but couldn't get it open.

Despairing, he waited for morning to come.

❖

Kevin couldn't sleep.

Everyone else in the Pit was tucked into bed. The light had gone out in Ford's room a half hour ago, and Gear was snoring through the walls. Mrs. Morris never snored, but Kevin was sure she was asleep with her black eye mask and the white noise machine she used to screen out irritations.

At first, he couldn't sleep because he'd been thinking about Danny. Danny, who was now officially not straight, but afraid to tell anyone. That sucked for him.

After that, he was thinking about Danny's silly questions. *How do you know there's not more to the story?* As if Ford or Gear or Mrs. Morris would ever keep information from him.

But maybe they didn't know, either.

Kevin went to the kitchen to get something to drink. After that, he drifted to the tech console, and then he tapped in a search or two.

He was ready to turn everything off and go to bed when he decided to check on the built-in GPS in Danny's phone.

It lit up on a map: the emergency room, Piedmont General Hospital.

On the phone, Danny insisted he was fine. A little ditch, a little accident. When he asked how Kevin knew, Kevin gave his own little white lie. He didn't think Danny would appreciate knowing there was a sensor in his phone, even if it was for his own good.

"Go home, stay safe, and stay out of trouble," Kevin told him, maybe more gruffly than he should.

Kevin double-checked the police scanner and reports to make sure the King wasn't involved. After that, he pulled up the record on Danny's phone since it had first been turned on. The map lit up, starting with Danny's house, then downtown, then up the hill with Mrs. Morris, then back to his house, and then to an address Kevin didn't recognize. After that, a meandering trail up to Moon Conway's mansion.

Kevin searched on the address. It was a rental. The owner lived in Knoxville, and there was no information on the current tenant.

How do you know there's not more to the story?

Kevin decided to get some fresh air.

❖

An old man was waiting for Kevin in the living room of the old Victorian house.

"You're rather young to be from the government," he said, his voice a rasp.

Kevin had found the house easily, hesitated only a little bit at the unlocked door, and then decided that he couldn't come this far and not go inside. The house was very quiet. He didn't see anything that would have brought Danny here until he got to this room, with its high ceilings and heavy drapes and electronic parts scattered everywhere.

The old man looked harmless enough, but thin and sickly. He reminded Kevin of someone who should be in the hospital, not staying up to greet midnight visitors. A tiny gold helicopter was hovering over his right shoulder, some kind of radio-controlled toy.

Like Danny's toy buggy, maybe. Kevin brought his FRED up to measure it. The helicopter beeped in alarm, then ducked behind the old man's armchair.

"Don't be silly," the old man said, coughing weakly. "He's not going to hurt you."

Kevin wasn't sure who he was trying to assure. "Who are you?"

"Eliot Beaudreau," the man replied. "Of Flint, Michigan. Be sure they spell that first name correctly. One t and one l only."

Kevin carefully scanned the rest of the room. Nothing showed up on his FRED. The helicopter peeked up over Beaudreau's shoulder, its blades whirring very quietly, but then ducked down again.

"Mr. Beaudreau, do you know what Ruins are?" Kevin asked.

Beaudreau choked for a moment. No, not choked. Laughed. Kevin's face burned.

"They're nothing to laugh about," Kevin said. "They kill people."

With a wave of his hand and a tight clutch on his handkerchief, the old man regained his composure.

"They're like people, boy. The bad ones kill innocent men, women, and children. The good ones try to stop them. Just like humans."

Now Kevin knew where Danny had gotten his questions. "You really believe that?" he asked skeptically.

"Believe it? I know it." The old man coughed again, a deep and unnerving hack. "I've been in the assembly plants. I worked the lines. For twenty years now, I've tried to get the government to listen to me, but all they have is suspicion and hate."

The helicopter had slowly elevated itself as Beaudreau spoke. Kevin could see that it had a small label on it: CHOPR. It was hovering near its owner's shoulder in a way that almost looked worried.

"I can see you don't believe me," Beaudreau said. "It isn't easy, disbelieving what you've been taught. But there are good Ruins just as surely as there are bad ones. I should know."

Kevin eyed the nearby doorways. "There are more here?" he asked warily. It suddenly occurred to him that this might be a big trap of some kind, and he'd walked right into it.

Beaudreau shook his head and rasped for enough air to speak. "I've sent them all away now. The end of our friendship has come."

That didn't sound good. In the dim light from one old lamp, Beaudreau's lips had taken on a blue tinge.

Reaching for his phone, Kevin said "I'm going to call the paramedics—"

"No," Beaudreau snapped, and CHOPR darted away in alarm. "Don't."

"Why not?" Kevin asked.

"What do I want machines and needles for?" Beaudreau asked. "I'm eighty years old. I'm ready."

"I still think—"

Beaudreau stiffened in the chair, his gaze sharp. "I'll tell you what to think. There's a King in town. You want him. I didn't have all the pieces when that other young man was here. But CHOPR…he put it together. Figured it out."

The helicopter settled back down by Beaudreau's shoulder and let out a plaintive beep. Kevin didn't think the old man had much time left. The force of his convictions was strong, like a tidal wave, but Kevin didn't want to be swayed. Couldn't be, not just because of one old man's opinion.

"Can you…" Beaudreau waved his fingers. "Oxygen. In the kitchen."

Kevin hurried into the kitchen. It was a mess in there, all sorts of junk and parts and old magazines, but he didn't see any oxygen tanks. When he returned to the living room, apologizing, he saw that Beaudreau had gone still and slack in his chair, his face empty of life.

CHOPR, now sitting on his shoulder, let out a sad little noise.

Kevin wasn't fooled. A toy helicopter was no more capable of feeling sad than was a wrench or a sofa or a forklift. But CHOPR gingerly nudged Beaudreau with its still tail, and when the old man didn't move, he let out another noise.

It wasn't the first time Kevin had been around a dead body, but it was maybe one of the most melancholy times—an old man with no nearby family or friends, this old house full of junk, a Ruin sitting on his shoulder—

Kevin lifted his FRED. CHOPR beeped, squeaked, and zipped over to the dining room table.

"I'm not going to—" Kevin started to say, because he wasn't going to fry him. He just wanted a good solid reading. CHOPR landed on the table for a brief moment, slid on a newspaper, then zoomed up to the ceiling and an open heating vent of some kind.

"Wait!" Kevin called out. "What did he mean, you figured it out?"

Too late. CHOPR was gone. The stray newspaper crunched under Kevin's boot and he looked down. The headlines jumped out at him: one about the teens who had crashed their car into an oncoming train and the other about Country Harvest.

The helicopter had figured it out.

And now Kevin did, too.

CHAPTER THIRTY-TWO

Mom was still mad at him. And she didn't want him out of her sight. But she couldn't skip her job today, so Danny was going to have to go to the fairgrounds with her.

"You can't!" he said, still lying in bed. "You know how much I hate country music! And it's my birthday. You can't torture me with country music on my birthday."

She picked up a pair of dirty jeans from the floor. "Here's how you can spend your birthday: figuring out how you're going to pay for the deductible on Eric's car repairs. His mom has already called asking about the money."

Danny winced. "What was I supposed to do? Let him drive drunk?"

"You're just lucky Roger convinced those police officers not to cite you for driving without a license, because otherwise your probation from California could be revoked."

At the bottom of the bed, Comet lifted his head.

Suspicious, Danny asked, "How'd he convince them of that?"

Mom was in his closet now, picking out clean clothes. "He had to give them two front-row tickets to Moon's concert at the Opry tonight."

"So it's okay to bribe the police?"

She emerged with jeans and a blue shirt. "Get up and get dressed. Roger already went ahead for the VIP breakfast, which I have to miss thanks to you. We leave in fifteen minutes."

"But I have a broken wrist!" he protested.

"Don't get the cast wet in the shower," she replied. On her way out of the room she nearly tripped. She cursed under her breath, leaned down, and picked up a toy fire truck. "And will you stop leaving these things around!"

Danny said, "But—" and then stopped himself.

He didn't own a fire truck. But Mr. Beaudreau did. This was the same one that had been in Beaudreau's house—a long ladder truck with the license plate FIREBUG mounted to its front fender.

Mom put it on the desk and left. Once she was gone, FIREBUG lit up and rolled back and forth.

"What are you doing here?" Danny asked it. "Did 2KEWLE send you?"

The truck's ladder swung around.

Danny said, "I can't go with you right now."

FIREBUG hooted its horn.

"I can't," Danny said. "I'll be grounded for life. You're just going to have to come with me."

Traffic to the fairgrounds was already thick at eight a.m., but there was a back road entrance for VIPs, and Mom had a pass that let them into a special parking area behind the main tent. Musicians, staging crew, and technicians were working hard together, and fans were already lined up outside the front.

"I have a book report to do," Danny said. "Can I just sit here and work on it?"

Mom looked suspicious at his newfound enthusiasm for homework. "You can sit backstage."

He followed her inside. The yellow skin of the tent stretched high above hundreds of seats. Moon Conway was standing on a large stage, testing out a microphone. He wore his traditional cowboy boots and an enormous white cowboy hat. Danny saw no sign of Junior, though surely he was around, too.

"Back there," Mom said, showing him a dirt-packed area where some sound equipment was still being unpacked. "Don't wander off without telling me."

"I won't," he mumbled.

"Look at me and say that again," Mom said sternly.

Danny lifted his chin. "I won't," he promised her.

Without good reason, he added silently to himself.

She sighed, shook her head, and went off to do her job. Once Danny was sure no one was watching him, he took FIREBUG out of his backpack. The ladder truck turned itself on, beeped once, and zapped Danny with a silver spark.

"Oww!" Danny said, dropping him. "What was that for?"

FIREBUG zoomed toward the nearest tent flap.

"No, wait!" Danny said.

He risked a glance toward Mom, but she was on stage with a clipboard in hand, giving information to a group of technicians.

Danny ducked out of the tent and followed FIREBUG.

CHAPTER THIRTY-THREE

Twenty thousand country-western fans had gathered on the sunny Piedmont Fairground. Kevin hated the dust, the squealing fans, and the rows of glittery booths where chirpy, bright-eyed hopefuls waited desperately for someone to recognize and adore them. He liked rock 'n' roll and always would, not this twanging, silly music for honky-tonk bars and rodeos.

But here he was, roaming the aisles, ignoring calls for free music samples and other worthless trinkets, not buying T-shirts or souvenir mugs, looking for the Ruin King.

Kevin's earpiece beeped. Mrs. Morris said, "I'm in the west lot. Nothing suspicious."

Gear reported in from the east lot. "Not here, either. This better not be a wild goose chase, kid."

Kevin didn't answer that. He'd had to use every bit of his persuasive skill to get the team to take his idea seriously: that Country Harvest would be a great place for a Ruin King to gather enough zorons for an Ignition. He didn't dare tell them about CHOPR. Not yet, at least. Mr. Boudreau's body hadn't even been discovered yet. Kevin would have to place an anonymous call to the police when this was over to make sure the elderly man got a decent burial.

Ford got on the radio. "Keep looking," he said. "This is as good a place as any."

The team wasn't searching alone, of course. Ford had called in dozens of Free Mechanics to lend assistance. They'd come from far and wide, scruffy men and women with grease under their fingernails and ball caps on their heads.

"If we don't stop it today, who knows how many people might die," Ford had told them.

The mechanics had spread out through the parking lots and fields of overflow parking, but Kevin didn't have much hope they'd find the King quickly. Not with thousands and thousands of cars, trucks, SUVs, vans, and motorcycles to hide in.

Not for the first time, Kevin wished there were fewer engines in the world.

A familiar face appeared in the crowd, heading for the barbeque pits. Kevin's heart sank. What was Danny doing here? Kevin broke into a sprint and caught up with him outside a lemonade stand.

"You should be home," Kevin snapped.

Danny gave a guilty start but kept walking. "What are you doing here?"

"My job," Kevin said. "Why are you—"

He stopped when he caught sight of what Danny was following: a little red fire truck, rolling along on the ground.

"Don't," Danny said, catching Kevin's arm before he could reach for his FRED. "It's trying to help. I know you don't think you can trust any of them, but this one's different."

The look on Danny's face was sincere and urgent. Kevin didn't have time to tell Danny about Mr. Beaudreau or CHOPR. Instead, he asked, "Where's it going?"

"I'm not sure," Danny said.

The festival booths and music tents had been set up in a giant horseshoe shape facing a Ferris wheel and carnival rides for little kids. FIREBUG led them past the western end of the horseshoe, beyond a barbeque pit and picnic area, and into a dusty field where hundreds of cars and trucks had been parked. The fire engine stopped.

Kevin asked, "What's it doing?"

"Looking for the King," Danny said. "He zapped me and I can see the colors again. All of these are purple—"

Kevin grabbed his FRED and his radio. The sensor readings blinked 85, 89, 95—

"Dad!" he said into his radio. "It's happening right now! The Ignition!"

❖

Danny scrambled up on the hood of a green Mazda Miata and scanned the field. He stepped over to a Lincoln Town Car. His vision started to blur. He thought he could hear a hum like a giant machine gearing up. Down on the ground, FIREBUG rolled along and tooted its horn.

An answering toot sounded from somewhere nearby.

Danny focused on a cherry red Corvette that looked purple in the sunlight. Buddy Hunt's car. The beeping from the trunk sounded just like 2KEWLE.

Kevin was yelling into his radio. "It's here! The west field—"

On the other side of the fairgrounds, Ford heard Kevin's frantic words. He started running.

Mrs. Morris was by the Ferris wheel, scanning an ice-cream truck. She, too, began running toward Kevin's position.

Gear, in the RV with the dogs, grabbed his equipment and dashed toward the west field.

None of them were going to make it in time.

CHAPTER THIRTY-FOUR

Danny jumped down to the ground and began tugging on the Corvette's trunk. Inside, 2KEWLE beeped frantically. The Corvette began rocking back and forth on its tires like a wild horse.

"Get back!" Kevin yelled. He aimed his FRED at the car. "I have to zap it!"

"Give me a minute!" Danny yelled back.

The hum got louder, rapidly escalating into a screech and irritating whine. Over at the barbeque pit, people began to point and take pictures with their phones. The Corvette rose several inches off the ground, but still Danny struggled to open the trunk. He couldn't just leave 2KEWLE inside. The front and back windshields both cracked vertically and the trunk popped open.

2KEWLE leapt up into Danny's arms.

Kevin fired his FRED.

The Corvette soared straight up into the clouds and imploded. Purple and gold shards of jagged lightning zigzagged through the sky. Danny felt himself thrown backward. He expected a shower of burning metal and gasoline, but there was only light, terrible and awful, and the sound of something like a great machine tearing itself to pieces.

Then he slammed into something unforgivably hard, and all sound and vision went away.

❖

Danny's ears rang with the painful reverberation of his heartbeat. It was a fast but steady rhythm, nothing he could put a melody to. Groggily, he pulled himself to his feet. 2KEWLE was still in his arms, looking singed and drained.

"Oh, no," he said.

He stumbled to his feet, shaking 2KEWLE. The buggy didn't respond. Danny tucked it under his arm and went in search of Kevin. He was sitting up groggily, blood streaming from a cut on the side of his head.

"Are you all right?" Danny asked.

Kevin said, "I think so."

Spectators and police began to gather close by. Danny heard sirens getting close. Ford, Gear, and Mrs. Morris arrived, out of breath and frantic.

"Are you hurt?" Ford demanded, dropping to Kevin's side.

"No," Kevin insisted. "I'm fine."

2KEWLE hadn't been the only casualty of the Ignition. Hundreds of cars across the lot had wisps of steam rising up from under their hoods. Several had flat tires or broken windows. Where the Corvette had been parked, there was only blackened grass and ash. Danny found FIREBUG as damaged and lifeless as 2KEWLE.

"Do they always fly into the sky like that?" Danny asked. His voice sounded weird in his own ears.

Gear was scanning the area with his FRED. "Not usually."

Mrs. Morris was sweeping the field as well. "Zero. All the zoron counts are zero."

"What does that mean, zero?" Danny asked.

Ford helped Kevin up. "It means the King sucked up all their energy and made it part of his own. It's an Ignition."

"But where is it now?" Danny asked.

None of them could answer.

All this destruction, and the King was still out there.

Before Danny could ask more, Mom and Roger Rat rushed over.

"Danny!" Mom examined his dirty cast and brushed dirt off his shoulders. "Are you okay?"

"I'm fine," he said miserably, holding 2KEWLE's hulk. "It was just an explosion."

"Just an explosion!" Her hands cupped his face. "What happened?"

"Someone said it was lightning," Mrs. Morris said helpfully.

"Lightning?" Roger looked up at the clear blue sky, bewildered. "How could it be lightning?"

"Weather can be very strange sometimes," Ford said, one hand on Kevin's shoulders. "Danny, I'm glad you're not hurt. We'll see you later."

Kevin looked back over his shoulder, his eyes imploring Danny to not say anything about Ruins. Morris and Gear followed silently, their FREDS tucked away.

"Come on, Danny," Mom said. "Let the police handle this."

She steered him away from the blistered field. He went, reluctantly, with 2KEWLE and FIREBUG tucked under his arms.

"Hey!" Buddy Hunt said, running past. "Where's my car?"

Kevin brushed Ford's hand aside. "I'm fine. Stop fussing!"

They were back in the Pit, which was parked behind the merry-go-round on the fairway. Mrs. Morris and Gear were sitting at the computer console, scanning the fairgrounds. Zeus and Apollo sat in the corner, looking alert. The first aid kit was wide open on the table beside Kevin.

"We should go to the hospital," Ford said.

"Dad, I don't even have a headache. I promise."

Ford sighed. He turned toward the console. "Anything?"

"Nothing," Mrs. Morris reported. "Not a trace."

Gear said, "It had to go somewhere. At the moment of Ignition, it jumped into something that's probably a lot bigger and a lot heavier. Where would you go if you were a Ruin King flush with new power?"

"Far from here," Kevin said.

"Check to see if the railroad runs nearby," Ford said. "Get the traffic cam for the highway. We're looking for anything big enough to snag its attention."

Kevin gazed out the window. His father was right, of course. Now that the King had power, it could wreak havoc with bigger and badder things than a red Corvette.

But what if it was still at Country Harvest, biding its time? Where would it hide?

Chapter Thirty-five

"Okay, here's the deal," Mom said. "You're going to sit right here backstage, where I can see you. Right after Moon's concert, I have to go with him to the Opry on the tour bus. When I leave, Roger will take you home, and tonight, we're going to have the longest talk in the history of long talks. I'm not sure I'm buying this lightning story at all."

They were backstage in the big tent again. The prospect of sticking around for a few more hours while thousands of fans adored Moon Conway didn't make Danny happy, but he didn't have the strength to argue.

"Okay," he said. "We'll talk."

Mom touched the side of his head. "You're sure you're okay? You're awfully quiet."

"I'm fine," he said. He sucked in a deep breath and steadied his shaking hands against his thighs. "I think, well, I think you should know. I'm gay."

Her eyebrows shot upward just as her mouth dropped open. It would have been comical, if it weren't the most important announcement of his life.

"Well," Mom said, "that's not what I expected you to say."

Danny's fingers had gone cold. He thought that was because all his blood was rushing around in anxiety. "That's it? I'm gay. I like boys."

"Yes, I know what it means," she said dryly. "This is definitely not the best time and place to talk about it, though, is it?"

"I guess not," he admitted.

Mom kissed his forehead. "I'm glad you told me. We'll talk later."

He sat backstage as promised. Stayed still, out of the way, talking to no one, while the concert hall gradually filled up. Mom was never far away. Fans filled all the bleachers wearing Moon T-shirts and carrying signs that said "WE LUV U MOON!" When the music started, it was loud and twangy and made Danny's head hurt, but he had worse pains to consider. Both 2KEWLE and FIREBUG were ruined chunks of metal, and the King was still loose.

"Hey," a voice said, and Danny turned to see Laura.

"Hey," he replied.

She was wearing a backstage pass like his. It flapped around her neck as she sat beside him. Out in the front part of the tent, Moon and his band began a slow ballad that had been a hit during the summer.

"My parents aren't happy about last night." Laura pulled on the pink sleeves of her sweater. "I told them it wasn't your fault, but they don't want me to hang out with you anymore."

Danny nodded, keeping his gaze elsewhere.

Mom, standing by the stage, looked over to check on him again.

Laura said, "I told them Rachel lied about the deer. Junior made you run off the road. Of all of us, you were the only one being responsible last night."

Danny looked over at her. Her pretty eyes were dark with regret. He knew that feeling all too well.

"I'm not always responsible," he said. "Two years ago in California, I was joyriding in a stolen car with a friend of mine, and we got into an accident. It was my fault. The judge dropped most of the charges as long as I agreed not to drive until I was twenty-one."

"Oh," she said.

"No one's supposed to be perfect," Danny said. "It's okay to mess up. But my mess-ups put people in danger."

"I don't think that's always true," Laura said. Her phone vibrated and she looked down at it. "That's my dad. I better go."

Danny stood up with her. "I lied last night," he said. "About the jock itch thing. I don't have it."

She tilted her head. "Why did you say it, then?"

"Because I wasn't ready," he said.

"Oh." Laura considered that for a moment. "Maybe I wasn't ready, either, which is why I had to drink all those beers to fortify myself. We can always, you know, later."

He took a deep breath. "I might not ever be ready. I mean, I know I won't. You're only the second person I've ever told this too, okay? But I think...you know."

Laura tilted her head. "Know what?"

"I like boys," Danny said.

Her reaction was a lot more extreme than Mom's.

"Are you kidding me?" she yelled, just as Moon's song ended, and the entire tent heard her. "You like *boys*?"

❖

"Well," Mom said tightly. "That was unexpected."

The crowd was leaving the tent, and the crew setting up for the next act. Moon had come off the stage drenched with sweat and surrounded by security. Roger was there too, of course, and he looked as unhappy as Mom did.

"I'll take care of things," he said to Mom. "I'll meet you at the Opry."

"Hurry," she said. To Danny she added, "And please don't make anyone else scream."

Danny, who figured he'd be grounded for *years*, only nodded. He wasn't sure, but he suspected his face was bright scarlet red and had been ever since Laura's indignant yelp. So much for small family secrets. By Monday, every single person at Piedmont would know the story.

Dazed, he followed Roger through the backstage maze to the VIP parking lot where Roger's Mercedes S350 was parked. Roger looked at him for a few moments, obviously trying to say something and not getting it out. When they were in the car, Roger turned on the ignition and turned it off again.

"Your mother says you think you're gay," Roger said.

Danny said nothing.

"She's worried about you," Roger said. "I'm worried too. If there's something you want to tell us, I want you know it's okay. If you got mixed up with the wrong people, if maybe there's drugs involved—"

"No!" Danny said. "There's no drugs."

Roger grimaced. "Well, of course you'll say that. But you know, when I was a kid, I maybe experimented a little—"

Danny wished he could sink through the car's floor and into the ground. He watched Moon Conway's forty-foot long tour bus start up. Moon's name and logo were painted in a glittery logo on the side. The bus itself was an unusual color.

"When did they paint the bus purple?" Danny asked.

Roger said, "It's not purple. It's silver."

Danny knew that. Because now that he was looking, he could see the purple was shifting and vibrating—almost like a thing alive.

The King.

Danny shouldered open the car door and started running.

CHAPTER THIRTY-SIX

The parking lot was jammed with rows of cars, trucks, and fans. Danny had to dodge around a cluster of autograph-seekers and sprint alongside the bus, which was picking up speed. He pounded on the door.

"Open up!" he shouted. "Hey! Open the door!"

The bus slowed. The pneumatic door hissed open, and Danny jumped in the stairwell. Buck Hamilton, the driver, peered at Danny in surprise from his leather bucket seat.

"What's wrong, kid?" he asked.

Danny liked Buck. They'd met at one of Roger's barbeques. Buck was at least sixty years old and wore a big old Stetson. Each year, he drove enough miles to go ten times around the world, or so he claimed.

"You have to stop the bus!" Danny said.

Buck didn't stop. Mom appeared in the aisle and said, "What the—Danny, what are you doing?"

"I've got to talk to you," he said.

"No! I'm busy."

"Everyone's got to get off the bus," Danny said. "It's not safe."

Buck steered out of the parking lot and on to the main road. "There's nothing wrong with my baby. I guarantee it."

Mom gave Danny a deadly glare, took him by the arm, and pulled him down the aisle. "Come back here."

The tour bus was opulent—sofas and flat-screen TVs, a galley kitchen stocked with refreshments, and additional compartments for the bathrooms and sleeping areas. Journalists with cameras and other recording devices were interviewing Moon in one area, and Junior and Rachel were sitting in bucket seats by the galley, arguing with each other.

"Because it's not right!" she was saying.

Junior broke off the fight to glare at Danny. "What's he doing here?"

Danny focused on Rachel. "All the trouble he caused and you go back to him?"

Mom yanked him into a small cabin that doubled as a bunkroom and office.

"Tell me what's going on," Mom said. "Why are you acting so crazy?"

"You won't believe me. But you have to trust me. There's something wrong with the bus. If we don't get it to stop, everyone could die." Danny opened his cell phone and hit the button for Kevin. When Kevin answered, he yelled, "It's here! On the bus!"

Kevin asked, "What? What bus?"

"Moon's tour bus!"

Mom demanded, "Who are you talking to?"

"You've got to make them stop," Kevin said.

"I'm trying," Danny said frantically. "Here, tell my mom."

He gave the phone to Mom and then hurried back to the cockpit. Traffic had momentarily slowed the bus, but a traffic officer motioned the bus toward an open lane.

"Buck, I'm not kidding. You've got to stop the bus and get everyone off," Danny said.

Buck looked irritated. "Kid, go back and sit down, will you? Get yourself some soda."

Junior came swaggering up the aisle. "Is he bothering you, Buck?"

"Shut up," Danny said.

"You shut up."

Rachel was close on Junior's heels. "What's going on here? Danny, are you going crazy?"

"All of you go sit down, will you?" Buck said. "You're distracting me."

Just then, the engine gave off a loud growling sound audible over over the sounds of Moon's interview with the journalists The bus lurched so hard that Rachel bounced into Junior and Junior nearly slammed up against Danny.

Junior demanded, "What was that?"

"Nothing!" Buck said. "Sit down!"

The steering wheel wrenched around in Buck's hands. This time the sharp swerve of the bus threw Danny, Junior, Rachel, and almost everyone else off balance. Moon Conway yelled, "What's going on up there?"

Buck had gone pale and sweaty in his seat. "I don't know! She's just—she's got a mind of her own!"

Danny grabbed one of the poles and pulled himself upright. He stared outside the windshield. For a moment, his eyes and his brain couldn't connect. He didn't understand what he was seeing. Cars, traffic lights, blue sky, the off ramp from I-65.

Off ramp. *Off.* And here they were, driving right up it.

❖

Back in the Pit, Kevin said, "The King is in Moon Conway's tour bus."

Ford asked, "What?"

Kevin gave the phone to his father and switched on the overhead monitors. The sensors tracked and focused on a long luxury coach just past the parking gates.

"Look at that zoron score," Mrs. Morris said. "Off the charts!"

Gear headed for the driver's seat. Kevin knew they didn't have much time. Neither Moon's tour bus nor the Pit were built for racing, and with the heavy Country Harvest traffic, it was going to be hard to catch up.

"Dad," Kevin said. "I've got to go help."

"No," Ford said. "It's too dangerous!"

Too late. Already, he was out the door. He circled around to the Pit's trailer and rolled the Kawasaki off the metal grating. As he slid on his helmet, he saw Ford reach for the handlebars of his Harley.

"We do it together," he said.

Kevin nodded. Father and son roared their motorcycles to life.

❖

"Wrong ramp," Danny said. "Buck, wrong ramp!"

"I can't stop her!" Buck yelled.

They had reached the highway and were plunging forward into the nearest lane of oncoming traffic. A Honda Civic swerved out of their way, blaring the horn. Danny had only a brief glimpse of the panicked driver before the Civic sideswiped a Toyota Corolla and both slammed into the median.

"Stop!" Junior and Rachel both yelled, as if that would help things.

Not only couldn't Buck stop the King, but it was obvious to Danny that Buck was having heart problems. His face had gone ash-gray and sweaty, and his right arm was hitched up as if filled with shooting pains. A moment later, Buck slumped over, unconscious.

"Help me!" Danny said to Junior.

Together, they got him out of the bucket seat and into the aisle. Rachel and Junior started pulling him back to one of the sofas.

Left alone, Danny tried everything he knew—the brakes, the emergency brakes, turning off the ignition—but nothing slowed the bus's wild ride. The speedometer needle swept upward. More horns blasted through the air as a gasoline tanker bore down on them. He'd read about a tanker somewhere that had flipped and exploded with such force that it melted the highway decks below and above it. Tankers carried sixty to eighty thousand gallons of gasoline, all ready to ignite at the slightest scrape of metal on asphalt.

"Stop this bus!" Moon yelled from the back.

"I'm trying!" Danny yelled back.

The gasoline tanker blasted its air horn and swerved so sharply it started skidding. Danny didn't see what happened next. He was too busy facing the next horror in the lanes in front of them: a big yellow bus full of Sunday school kids.

Mom staggered her way up the aisle with Kevin's phone pressed to her ear. She stood in the stairwell, next to Danny. "It's some woman named Mrs. Morris. She says try to keep the bus in one lane! They're clearing traffic up ahead."

"I'm trying," Danny said through gritted teeth. "Mom, help me!"

Together, they tried to turn the wheel. The Ruin King wasn't giving them any purchase at all. The school bus managed to swerve away, but behind it were more cars and trucks. Danny couldn't bear to think about the innocent drivers who were about to get killed. Moms and dads, babies, grandparents. He'd always hated the driver who'd killed his dad and Mickey, but here he was, about to be just like him.

Two motorcycles roared up alongside the bus: a Harley low rider and a Kawasaki. Ford and Kevin.

"Tell them to zap us!" Danny said. "Otherwise, we're going to kill a lot of people."

Mom relayed the instructions, and said, "She says they can't do it with so many people onboard."

"They have to!" Danny said.

The tour bus veered across another lane, right into the path of a tractor-trailer carrying a dozen brand new cars. The reporters screamed. At the same time, the pneumatic controls on the door hissed and the door started to open.

The engine gunned. The speedometer swung past eighty miles an hour and made a fast approach to ninety.

Crouched over Buck's body, Rachel said, "We're going to die!"

The bus swerved again.

And Mom, trapped in the stairwell, started falling toward the highway.

❖

Danny shouted, "No!" but it was too late. Mom was falling and she was going to land hard on the asphalt at ninety miles an hour, her body broken beyond repair.

She was only inches from death when a hand reached out and saved her. Junior hooked his hand on the back of her slacks and hauled her back inside.

"Are you okay?" Danny demanded.

"I'm fine," Mom gasped.

In the lanes up ahead, police cruisers with spinning lights were stopping traffic. Kevin's team must have alerted the highway patrol. Motorcycle cops were throwing long black strips across the asphalt.

Rachel staggered forward. "What are they doing?"

"Spike strips," Junior said.

Danny didn't think blowing out the tires would help. The Ruin would just keep going on the rims. That's what happened with all the car chases he'd seen in California. Or the Ruin would swerve into a lane of stopped traffic, resulting in devastating carnage.

Outside the bus door, Kevin and Ford were arguing over their radios. Ford apparently had reached the same conclusion as Danny and was lifting his FRED.

The King in the engine roared and the speedometer swung upward again.

Danny saw everything very clearly now. He saw that the situation was helpless. They were all going to die, one way or another. The King was going to win. He also saw a glimpse of blue just off the highway.

They don't like water, Mr. Beaudreau had said.

"Help me," he said to Mom and Junior and Rachel. "Pull the wheel. Aim for that lake!"

"Are you crazy?" Junior demanded.

Mom, however, didn't hesitate. "Do it!"

The four of them tugged and pulled. Danny felt the muscles in his arm burn under the strain and his broken wrist, under the cast, made a noise that didn't sound good at all. If they didn't get over to the number one lane in the next fifteen seconds, they were going to smash right into a—

"Turn it!" he shouted.

They heaved the wheel clockwise. Moon Conway's very expensive bus swerved violently, smashed into the guardrail, and went sailing into the air.

Danny heard shouts and yelling and saw his mother standing white-knuckled with her arms wrapped around the stairwell pole. Junior tried to hold Mom and Rachel both. The reporters screamed, and Moon yelled, and the bus sailed through the air in no particular hurry.

Then they hit the lake and the steering wheel came up to slam against Danny's face.

CHAPTER THIRTY-SEVEN

Kevin had no idea what Danny was doing. One moment, Moon Conway's bus was barreling toward a collision course with the spike strips. The next, it was punching through the guardrail and sailing across the sky toward a very large body of water.

He heard the rest of the team swearing over his headset.

"Is he crazy?" Mrs. Morris asked.

"I'm going to kill him myself," Ford said.

The bus came down hard in the lake. Kevin braked to a screeching stop and tore off his helmet. He expected the bus to sink immediately, but the water only came up to the top of its tire rims.

The shallow end. That's what Danny had steered into.

He whooped for joy and slip-slid-ran down the slope into the cold, murky water. Behind him, cops and highway troopers began their own descent. A fire engine screeched to a stop, followed shortly by the Pit.

The rear exit of the tour bus popped open as Kevin and Ford reached the bus. Moon, Rachel, and the reporters jumped down into the water with shouts of dismay. The front door would open only a little bit against the mud, and Kevin wished he'd brought a crowbar. He dug his gloved hands into the opening and pulled. Ford leaned both of his hands and strength to the effort. On the other side, Junior pushed and used his shoulder to push some more.

They got the door open enough for Junior to say, "She's hurt. Danny, too."

The bus's engine revved. The Ruin, with its vast power, was trying to unstick itself from the mud. Any minute now, it might surrender the machine instead and jump its way back to the highway, maybe into a fire engine or another bus.

Ford helped Danny's mom out. She was saying, "No, I want to stay—" but it was clear that she had broken her arm, and there was a bleeding gash on her forehead.

Junior squeezed out behind her and said, "Danny's stuck."

Ford said, "Take them to the highway—" but Kevin was already wedging himself through the opening.

"I'll get Danny," he said. "You get them to safety, Dad."

"Kevin!" Ford yelled.

"It'll be okay," Kevin said. "We'll be right out."

Kevin hurried up the stairwell. Danny was leaning back in the driver's seat, blood coming from his nose. The airbag in the steering wheel had deployed and then deflated. It sagged over the steering wheel like a sad, punctured balloon.

"I think my noth ith broken," Danny said.

"You can have it fixed," Kevin said, relief almost making him dizzy. He bent over the driver, who was sprawled in the aisle. "Is anyone left onboard?"

"I don't think tho," Danny said. "How ith Buck?"

Kevin took a look at the angle of Buck's neck and shook his head.

"He's dead," he said, returning to the steering wheel. "Can you get up?"

He shook his head. "Stuck."

The steering column had dropped and jammed. The wheel was tight against his lap. No matter how hard Kevin tugged, it wouldn't move. They were going to need a winch and chain for that.

"Sorry," Danny said.

The engine was really whining now, and a thick smoke was beginning to roll past the galley and the leather seats. Kevin gulped hard and pulled his FRED out of his pocket.

He held the phone to the ignition and hesitated. "Kings don't die easily," he said.

Danny peered at him with bleary eyes. The blood from his nose was thick and bright red.

"Do it," he said and grabbed Kevin's free hand.

"Kevin!" Dad yelled from outside. "Don't!"

Kevin pressed the button.

Chapter Thirty-eight

The news was playing on the overhead television the second time Danny woke up.

He didn't remember much about the first time because the doctors had pumped him full of happy drugs. He knew his mother and Roger Rat had been there. His nose hurt and his wrist hurt and a lot of the rest of him hurt, too.

"You're going to be fine," Mom had said. She had one of those funny white braces on her neck and a cast on her arm. "You hear me, Danny? Just fine."

Then she burst into tears, which didn't reassure him at all.

Roger Rat patted her shoulder. "It's all right, Danny," he said. "Go back to sleep."

The second time was better. He didn't feel so fuzzy, no one was crying over him, and the TV was showing a documentary on Bruce Springsteen. Danny was desperately thirsty, but when he reached for the cup of water on the side table, he almost knocked it over.

"Careful!" a voice warned him.

He turned his head, slowly, because it seemed like he had one of those braces on, too. He hoped to see Kevin sitting there. Instead, it was Eric.

"Do you need something?" Eric asked.

"Water," Danny croaked out.

"Prima donna hero," Eric muttered. He got the cup and even held it for him while Danny sipped through the straw.

The water tasted delicious. It helped clear out the taste of smoke lingering at the back of Danny's mouth. He blinked several times at the new cast on his wrist and at the rest of his body, which seemed fine under a long white sheet.

"Your parents are in the cafeteria," Eric said. "There are reporters in the hallway and a security guard, too, because you're just so popular everyone wants to bust in here and grab an interview for the big story. *People* magazine, buddy. CNN."

Danny squinted at him. Eric never used to talk that quickly. Or maybe that was painkillers dulling Danny's brain.

"Crash?" he asked. "What big story?"

Eric gave him a sideways look. "You know. The bus driver had a heart attack behind the wheel, and drove on the highway on the wrong ramp, and somehow the steering and braking system failed, but you got behind the wheel and saved everyone."

Danny frowned. "That's the story?"

"Isn't it?"

"What about the other kid?" Danny asked. "In the bus with me. Kevin."

Eric frowned. "I don't know about any other kid. Who's Kevin?"

Mom came back just then. She no longer had the neck brace on, but there were dark circles under her eyes. She sent Eric off on an errand and sat down carefully by the side of his bed.

"How do you feel?" she asked.

"I'm okay," Danny croaked out. "Are you?"

She reached for his hand and squeezed it. "A lot better than I was, now that you're awake."

Danny felt his eyes well up a little. He hadn't meant to worry her, not about any of it. "Mom," he said. "I'm not crazy. I haven't been doing drugs or anything."

"I know," she said.

He blinked in disbelief. "Know what?"

"A man named Mr. Ford was here," she said. "He made me sign a bunch of papers about classified information and state secrets. Everyone else was told some cover story about Buck and a transmission problem."

"Oh." Danny felt relieved. "So you know."

"All about Ruins and Kings," Mom said. "But I can't tell Roger, which is very hard. When you love someone, you want to tell him everything. Especially about things that might hurt them."

Danny squeezed her hand. "At least we can tell each other."

She leaned over and kissed his forehead.

Danny suddenly couldn't keep his eyes open. "Is Kevin here? I want to see him."

"Who's Kevin?"

"He works with them," Danny said. "Ford and the others."

"Honey, no," Mom said.

And that's how he learned that Ford and his team had already left town without leaving any message at all for Danny.

EPILOGUE

It was a cold Saturday afternoon, just a few days after Danny's release from the hospital. He was supposed to be resting, but he'd dug his bicycle out of the garage and pedaled here, to Mr. Beaudreau's house, with his knapsack bulging on his back. The house was empty and had a *For Rent* sign on it.

"The old man?" a neighbor said. "He died. Sorry."

Danny felt like he'd been kicked in the stomach.

"Where'd all his stuff go?" he asked.

"Big moving truck took it away," the neighbor said. "No name on the truck."

Danny stared at the house for a while, wondering what he was supposed to do next. Then a quiet buzzing noise made him look skyward. A tiny gold helicopter zipped toward him, bearing the label CHOPR. After a moment, it darted away. Returned, flew away. Finally, Danny figured out it wanted him to follow it, and he pedaled all the way downtown with it leading the way.

Not far from Zinc's Sandwich Shop was a hobby store. Nicholas Toys. Danny remembered the name. It was the same store that Eric's sister used. An elderly black man was behind the counter, picking out a blues tune on an acoustic guitar. Danny knew that song. His dad had liked to play it, over and over.

"Good job, CHOPR," the old man said, putting aside the guitar. "Nice of you to finally come calling, Danny."

"Have we met?" Danny asked.

The old man shook his head. "Call me Nick. My friend Eliot Beaudreau, he said you had Detroit in your blood. Same way he did, same way I do."

Danny unzipped his backpack and pulled out the singed husks of 2KEWLE and FIREBUG. "Can you fix them?"

Nick closed the shop door, locked it, and pulled down the yellowed shade of the window. He carefully examined the two toys. Eventually, he said, "They're very badly damaged. Even if I could repair the circuit boards and motors, the Ruins that were in them are long gone. They might not ever come back."

"You could try, right?" Danny asked.

"My eyes aren't so good anymore," Nick said, tapping his thick eyeglasses. "I don't know if I can do the work."

Danny patted 2KEWLE. "But you could teach me, couldn't you?"

Nick smiled toothlessly. "Yes, I could. I could indeed."

❖

For the next two weeks, Danny was the most popular kid at school. The national news media covered the story of Moon Conway's runaway bus. Some of the reporters had captured the amazing light show as the King got zapped, but that had been written off as a freak problem with the bus's electrical system. Danny had checked carefully, and there was no mention of Ruins or car-possessing aliens anywhere in the news. He turned down interview requests and refused to talk about the incident at school. Eventually, people stopped asking.

That didn't stop them from gossiping about him, though. Danny Kelly, that gay kid. That's what happened when you grew up in San Francisco, someone whispered in class. No one had come up to him and tried to pick a fight or anything, but he'd be ready if they did. He felt bad about Laura, who alternated between shunning him and giving him dirty looks, but at least Eric was cool about it and some kids from the school's Rainbow Club had approached him about joining.

Now it was almost Thanksgiving. Danny was in the garage studio, plucking his guitar. With his wrist still in a cast, it was impossible to play chords, but he could still pick out notes one by one. He had in mind a song about his dad. A song he'd never tried to write before, but maybe it was time.

He was working on lyrics when he heard a sound downstairs. Outside the windows, dusk was coming on and the wind stirred leaves on the street.

Carefully, he padded down the steps. The lights over MUZKBUX were off, leaving everything in shadows.

"Who's there?" he asked, reaching for the light switch.

Kevin's hand reached the switch first and light flooded through the space. "Just me."

Danny blinked at him. "I've left you like a dozen messages, you jerk."

"I was in the hospital," Kevin said. "Under an alias. Kind of laid up for a while."

Up close, Danny could see that Kevin had dark circles under his eyes, and had lost some weight, and was leaning carefully on one leg.

"You're okay now?" Danny asked, his anger forgotten. He touched Kevin's hand, relishing the warm skin.

"Yeah," Kevin said. "But we're leaving town. New job, down in Austin. Another King."

Danny looked at him squarely. "Take me with you."

Kevin blinked in surprise. "What? No."

"I read more about my dad's accident," Danny said. "The police ruled out the other driver, and my dad, and any kind of mechanical failure. Just one of those things, they said. But it was a Ruin, wasn't it?"

Kevin asked, "Does it matter?"

"Yes!" Danny said. "I want to help stop these things. Ruins seem to like me for some reason. I can help you track them down faster."

He didn't say, *I've got Detroit blood.*

Kevin shook his head. "You have to graduate high school before the government will let you help."

"You didn't."

"Mrs. Morris homeschooled me and then I got my GED," Kevin said. "This job—it's not safe. I don't want to see you get hurt."

"And I don't want to see you get hurt, either," Danny said. "But it's kind of too late for that."

Kevin didn't answer. He glanced over his shoulder. Through the windows of the garage door, Danny could see the Pit parked at the curb. Ford was there, no doubt, as well as Gear and Mrs. Morris. Waiting for Kevin to rejoin their mission.

"You changed my life," Danny said. "You just can't leave me behind now."

He stepped forward and kissed Kevin. Right on the mouth, hard and hot, his hands gripping Kevin's shoulders tightly. It was everything that kissing Laura wasn't. It made Danny's whole body ache for more, *more right now*. And Kevin responded with the same kind of urgency mixed with sweetness, a kiss that promised all sorts of things Danny had dreamed about but never done.

But then Kevin broke it off and gave Danny a very slight smile. Pleased, but resigned as well.

He said, "I like your argument. Call me when you graduate."

And then he walked back to the RV, gave him a brief wave, and rode right out of Danny's life.

Part of Danny screamed at him to follow and ride off into the sunset. But he didn't move.

Two years until he graduated. Maybe he'd wait that long.

Or maybe he wouldn't.

"You can come out now," he called out.

2KEWLE and FIREBUG rolled out from under a workbench. CHOPR whirled down from the top of a cabinet. All three machines beeped their horns and flashed their lights.

"I know," Danny said. "We've got work to do."

THE END

About the Author

A Navy veteran, Sam Cameron spent several years serving in the Pacific and along the Atlantic coast. Her novels and short stories have been recognized for their wit, inventiveness, and passion. She holds an MFA in creative writing and currently teaches college in Florida.

Soliloquy Titles From Bold Strokes Books

The You Know Who Girls by Annameekee Hesik. As they begin freshman year, Abbey Brooks and her best friend, Kate, pinky swear they'll keep away from the lesbians in Gila High, but Abbey already suspects she's one of those you-know-who girls herself and slowly learns who her true friends really are. (978-1-60282-754-7)

In Stone by Jeremy Jordan King. A young New Yorker is rescued from a hate crime by a mysterious someone who turns out to be more of a something. (978-1-60282-761-5)

Wonderland by David-Matthew Barnes. After her mother's sudden death, Destiny Moore is sent to live with her two gay uncles on Avalon Cove, a mysterious island on which she uncovers a secret place called Wonderland, where love and magic prove to be real. (978-1-60282-788-2)

Another 365 Days by KE Payne. Clemmie Atkins is back, and her life is more complicated than ever! Still madly in love with her girlfriend, Clemmie suddenly finds her life turned upside down with distractions, confessions, and the return of a familiar face… (978-1-60282-775-2)

The Secret of Othello by Sam Cameron. Florida teen detectives Steven and Denny risk their lives to search for a sunken NASA satellite—but under the waves, no one can hear you scream… (978-1-60282-742-4)

Andy Squared by Jennifer Lavoie. Andrew never thought anyone could come between him and his twin sister, Andrea… until Ryder rode into town. (978-1-60282-743-1)

Sara by Greg Herren. A mysterious and beautiful new student at Southern Heights High School stirs things up when students start dying. (978-1-60282-674-8)

Boys of Summer, edited by Steve Berman. Stories of young love and adventure, when the sky's ceiling is a bright blue marvel, when another boy's laughter at the beach can distract from dull summer jobs. (978-1-60282-663-2)

Street Dreams by Tama Wise. Tyson Rua has more than his fair share of problems growing up in New Zealand—he's gay, he's falling in love, and he's run afoul of the local hip-hop crew leader just as he's trying to make it as a graffiti artist. (978-1-60282-650-2)

me@you.com by KE Payne. Is it possible to fall in love with someone you've never met? Imogen Summers thinks so because it's happened to her. (978-1-60282-592-5)

Swimming to Chicago by David-Matthew Barnes. As the lives of the adults around them unravel, high school students Alex and Robby form an unbreakable bond, vowing to do anything to stay together—even if it means leaving everything behind. (978-1-60282-572-7)

365 Days by KE Payne. Life sucks when you're seventeen years old and confused about your sexuality, and the girl of your dreams doesn't even know you exist. Then in walks sexy new emo girl, Hannah Harrison. Clemmie Atkins has exactly 365 days to discover herself, and she's going to have a blast doing it! (978-1-60282-540-6)

Cursebusters! by Julie Smith. Budding psychic Reeno is the most accomplished teenage burglar in California, but one tiny screw-up and poof!—she's sentenced to Bad Girl School. And that isn't even her worst problem. Her sister Haley's dying of an illness no one can diagnose, and now she can't even help. (978-1-60282-559-8)

Who I Am by M.L. Rice. Devin Kelly's senior year is a disaster. She's in a new school in a new town, and the school bully is making her life miserable—but then she meets his sister Melanie and realizes her feelings for her are more than platonic. (978-1-60282-231-3)

Sleeping Angel by Greg Herren. Eric Matthews survives a terrible car accident only to find out everyone in town thinks he's a murderer—and he has to clear his name even though he has no memories of what happened. (978-1-60282-214-6)

Mesmerized by David-Matthew Barnes. Through her close friendship with Brodie and Lance, Serena Albright learns about the many forms of love and finds comfort for the grief and guilt she feels over the brutal death of her older brother, the victim of a hate crime. (978-1-60282-191-0)